EOIN COLFER

ARTEMIS FOWL

THE GRAPHIC NOVEL

Adapted by **Michael Moreci**

Art by **Stephen Gilpin**

DISNEP • HYPERION

Los Angeles   New York

CHAPTER ONE

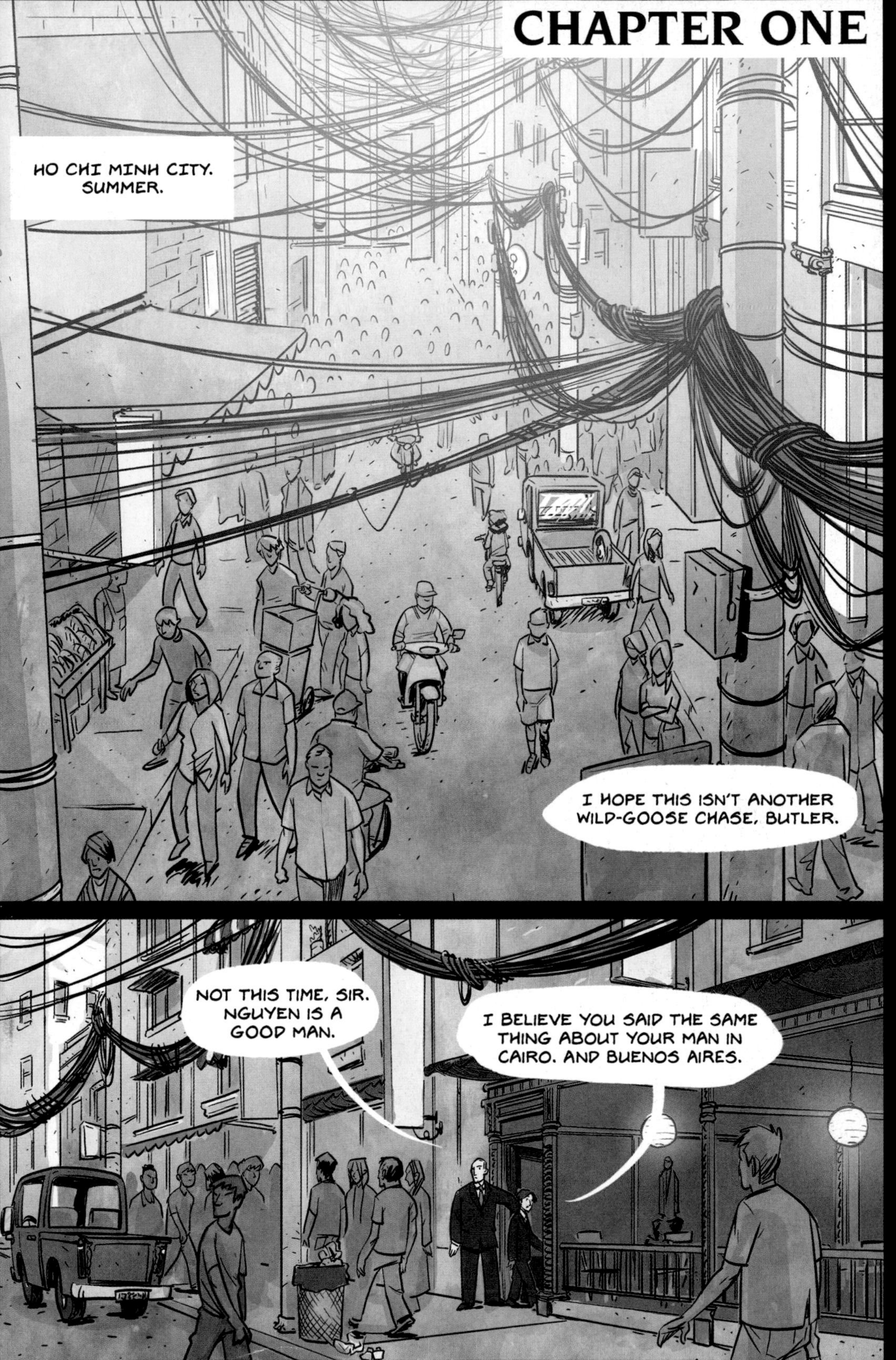
HO CHI MINH CITY.
SUMMER.
I HOPE THIS ISN'T ANOTHER WILD-GOOSE CHASE, BUTLER.
NOT THIS TIME, SIR. NGUYEN IS A GOOD MAN.
I BELIEVE YOU SAID THE SAME THING ABOUT YOUR MAN IN CAIRO. AND BUENOS AIRES.

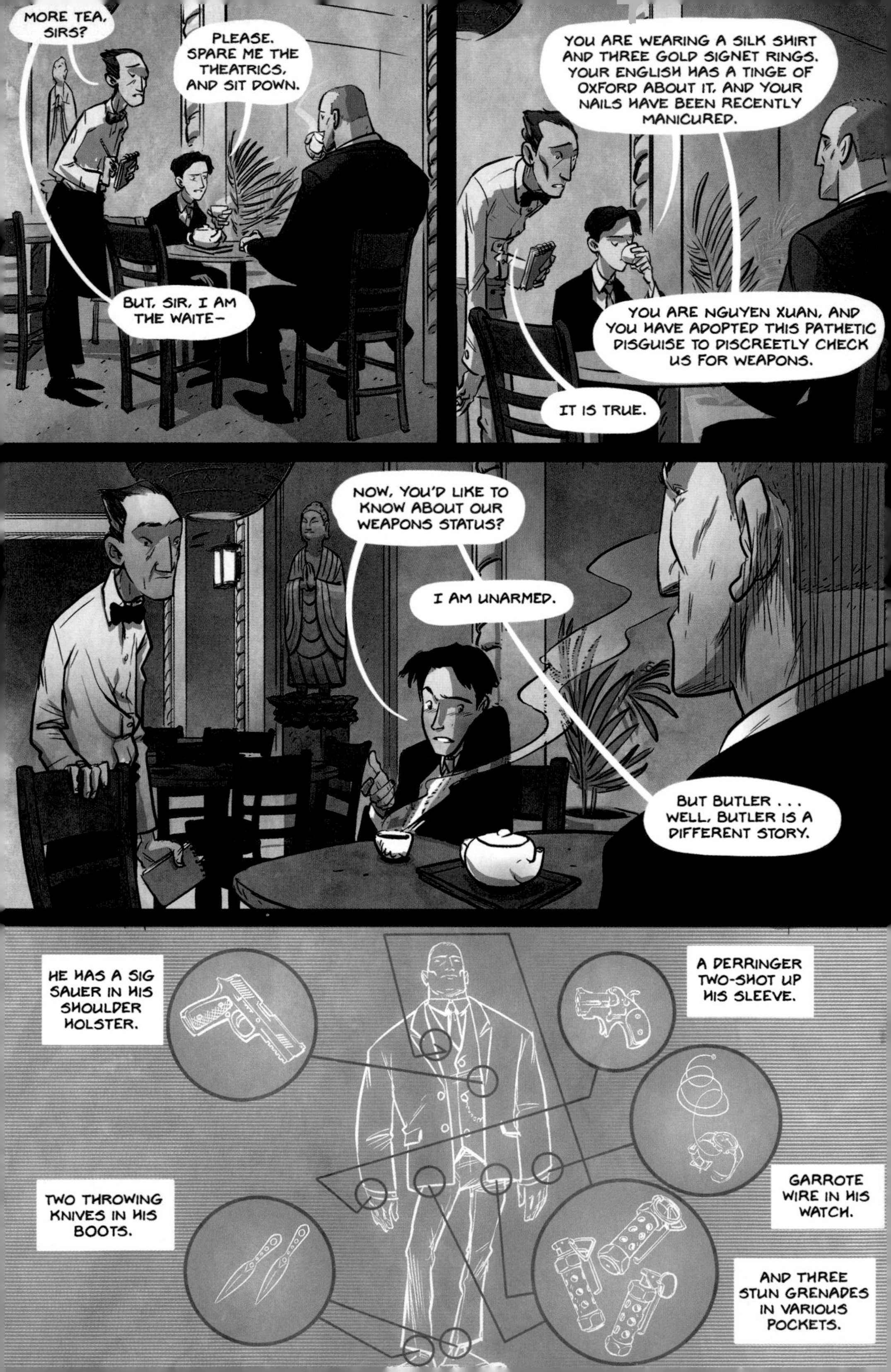
MORE TEA, SIRS?
PLEASE. SPARE ME THE THEATRICS, AND SIT DOWN.
BUT, SIR, I AM THE WAITE—
YOU ARE WEARING A SILK SHIRT AND THREE GOLD SIGNET RINGS. YOUR ENGLISH HAS A TINGE OF OXFORD ABOUT IT, AND YOUR NAILS HAVE BEEN RECENTLY MANICURED.
YOU ARE NGUYEN XUAN, AND YOU HAVE ADOPTED THIS PATHETIC DISGUISE TO DISCREETLY CHECK US FOR WEAPONS.
IT IS TRUE.
NOW, YOU'D LIKE TO KNOW ABOUT OUR WEAPONS STATUS?
I AM UNARMED.
BUT BUTLER . . . WELL, BUTLER IS A DIFFERENT STORY.
HE HAS A SIG SAUER IN HIS SHOULDER HOLSTER.
A DERRINGER TWO-SHOT UP HIS SLEEVE.
GARROTE WIRE IN HIS WATCH.
TWO THROWING KNIVES IN HIS BOOTS.
AND THREE STUN GRENADES IN VARIOUS POCKETS.

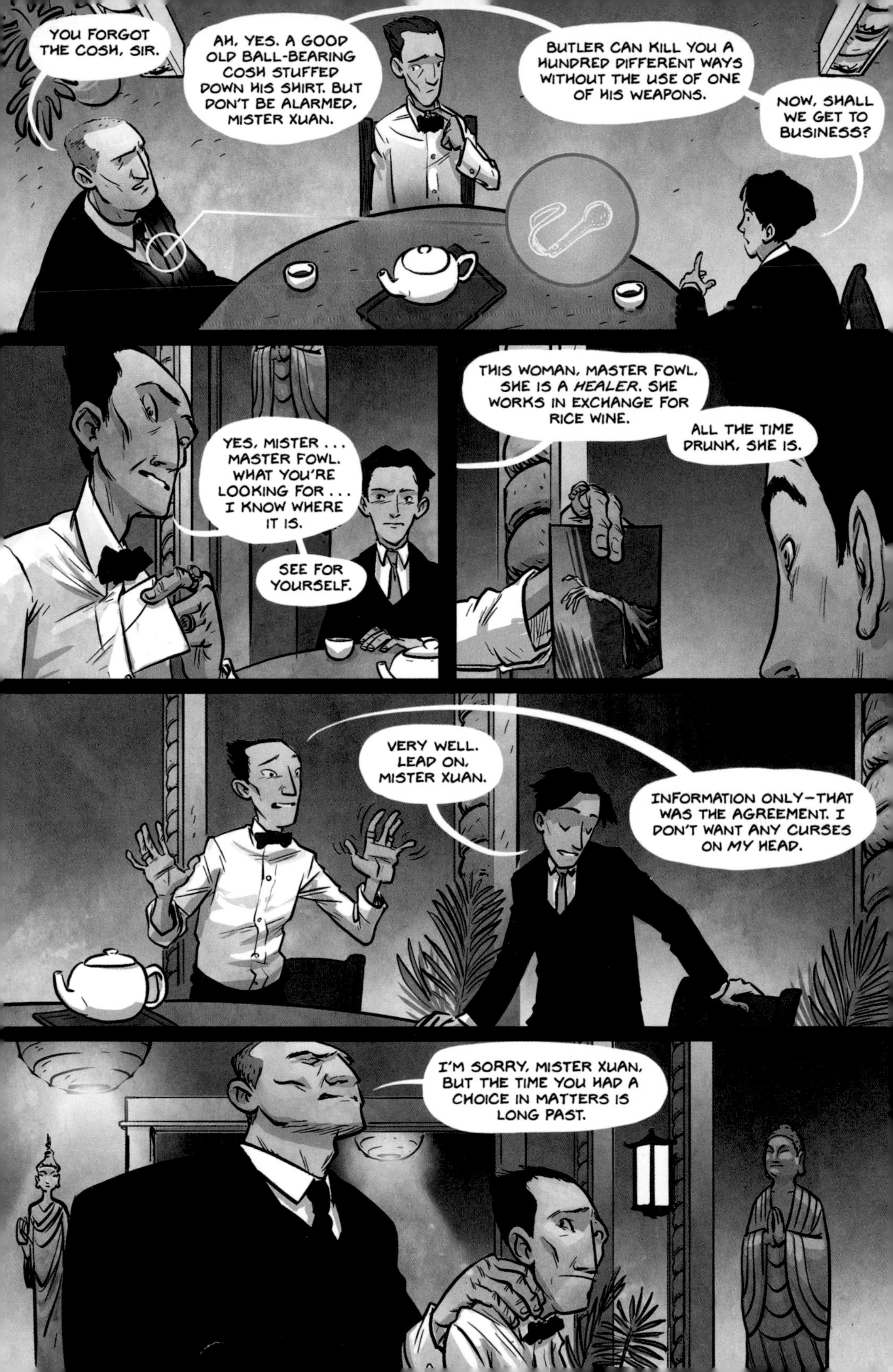
YOU FORGOT THE COSH, SIR.
AH, YES. A GOOD OLD BALL-BEARING COSH STUFFED DOWN HIS SHIRT. BUT DON'T BE ALARMED, MISTER XUAN.
BUTLER CAN KILL YOU A HUNDRED DIFFERENT WAYS WITHOUT THE USE OF ONE OF HIS WEAPONS.
NOW, SHALL WE GET TO BUSINESS?
YES, MISTER . . . MASTER FOWL. WHAT YOU'RE LOOKING FOR . . . I KNOW WHERE IT IS.
SEE FOR YOURSELF.
THIS WOMAN, MASTER FOWL, SHE IS A *HEALER*. SHE WORKS IN EXCHANGE FOR RICE WINE.
ALL THE TIME DRUNK, SHE IS.
VERY WELL. LEAD ON, MISTER XUAN.
INFORMATION ONLY—THAT WAS THE AGREEMENT. I DON'T WANT ANY CURSES ON *MY* HEAD.
I'M SORRY, MISTER XUAN, BUT THE TIME YOU HAD A CHOICE IN MATTERS IS LONG PAST.

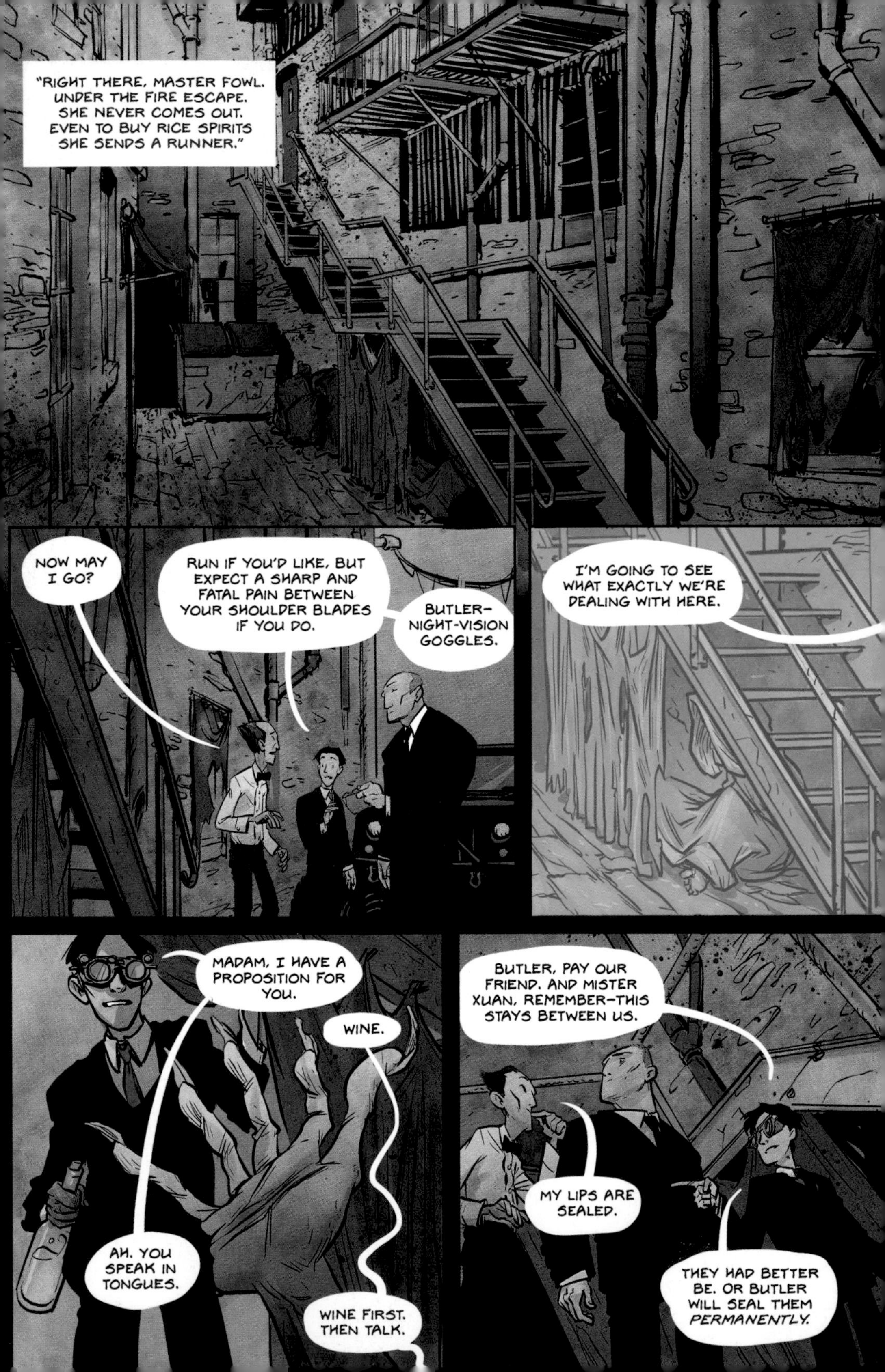
"RIGHT THERE, MASTER FOWL. UNDER THE FIRE ESCAPE. SHE NEVER COMES OUT. EVEN TO BUY RICE SPIRITS SHE SENDS A RUNNER."
NOW MAY I GO?
RUN IF YOU'D LIKE, BUT EXPECT A SHARP AND FATAL PAIN BETWEEN YOUR SHOULDER BLADES IF YOU DO.
BUTLER– NIGHT-VISION GOGGLES.
I'M GOING TO SEE WHAT EXACTLY WE'RE DEALING WITH HERE.
MADAM, I HAVE A PROPOSITION FOR YOU.
WINE.
AH. YOU SPEAK IN TONGUES.
WINE FIRST. THEN TALK.
BUTLER, PAY OUR FRIEND. AND MISTER XUAN, REMEMBER–THIS STAYS BETWEEN US.
MY LIPS ARE SEALED.
THEY HAD BETTER BE. OR BUTLER WILL SEAL THEM *PERMANENTLY.*

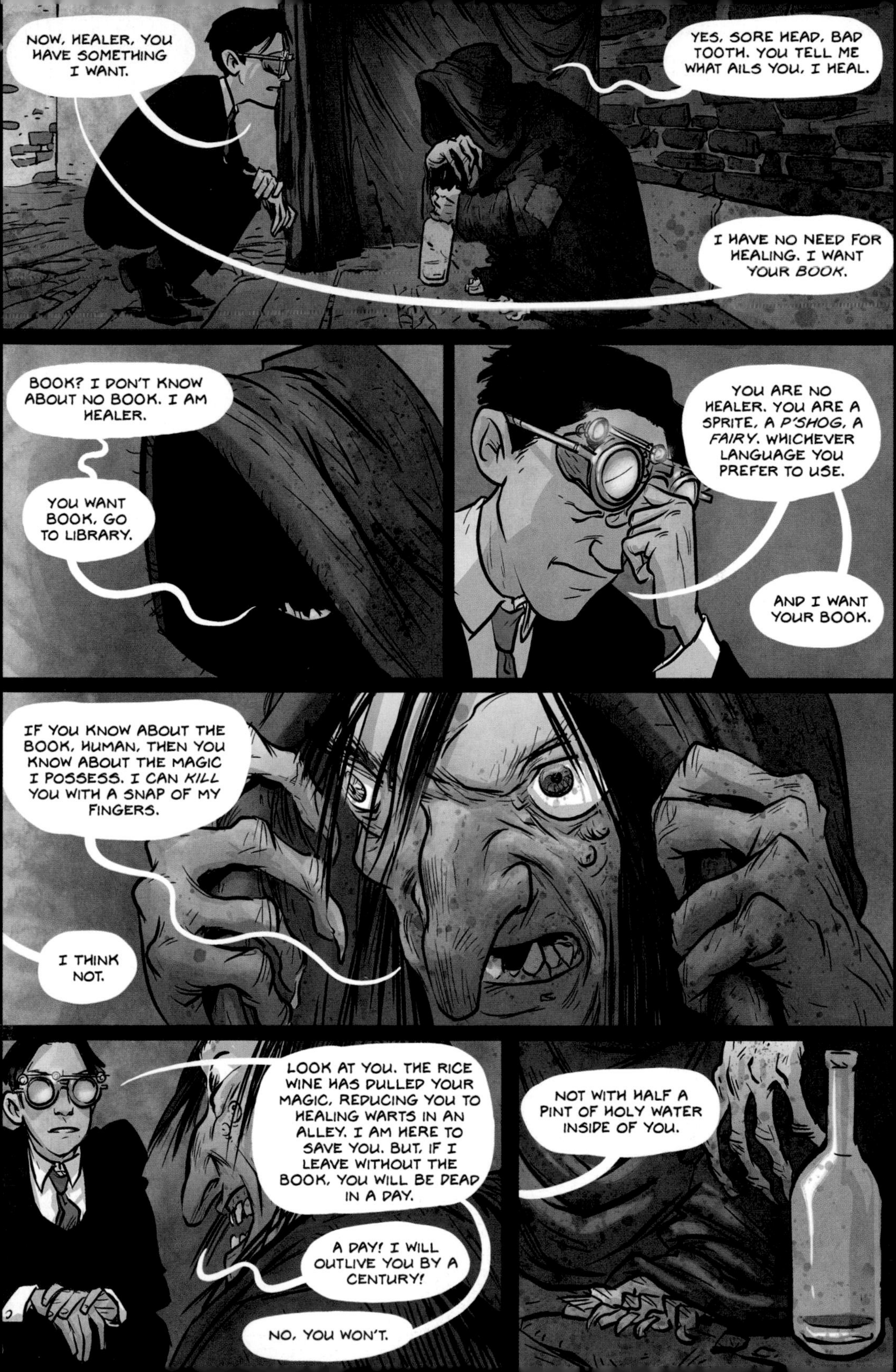
NOW, HEALER, YOU HAVE SOMETHING I WANT.
YES, SORE HEAD, BAD TOOTH. YOU TELL ME WHAT AILS YOU, I HEAL.
I HAVE NO NEED FOR HEALING. I WANT YOUR *BOOK*.
BOOK? I DON'T KNOW ABOUT NO BOOK. I AM HEALER.
YOU WANT BOOK, GO TO LIBRARY.
YOU ARE NO HEALER. YOU ARE A SPRITE, A *P'SHOG*, A *FAIRY*. WHICHEVER LANGUAGE YOU PREFER TO USE.
AND I WANT YOUR BOOK.
IF YOU KNOW ABOUT THE BOOK, HUMAN, THEN YOU KNOW ABOUT THE MAGIC I POSSESS. I CAN *KILL* YOU WITH A SNAP OF MY FINGERS.
I THINK NOT.
LOOK AT YOU. THE RICE WINE HAS DULLED YOUR MAGIC, REDUCING YOU TO HEALING WARTS IN AN ALLEY. I AM HERE TO SAVE YOU. BUT, IF I LEAVE WITHOUT THE BOOK, YOU WILL BE DEAD IN A DAY.
A DAY! I WILL OUTLIVE YOU BY A CENTURY!
NO, YOU WON'T.
NOT WITH HALF A PINT OF HOLY WATER INSIDE OF YOU.

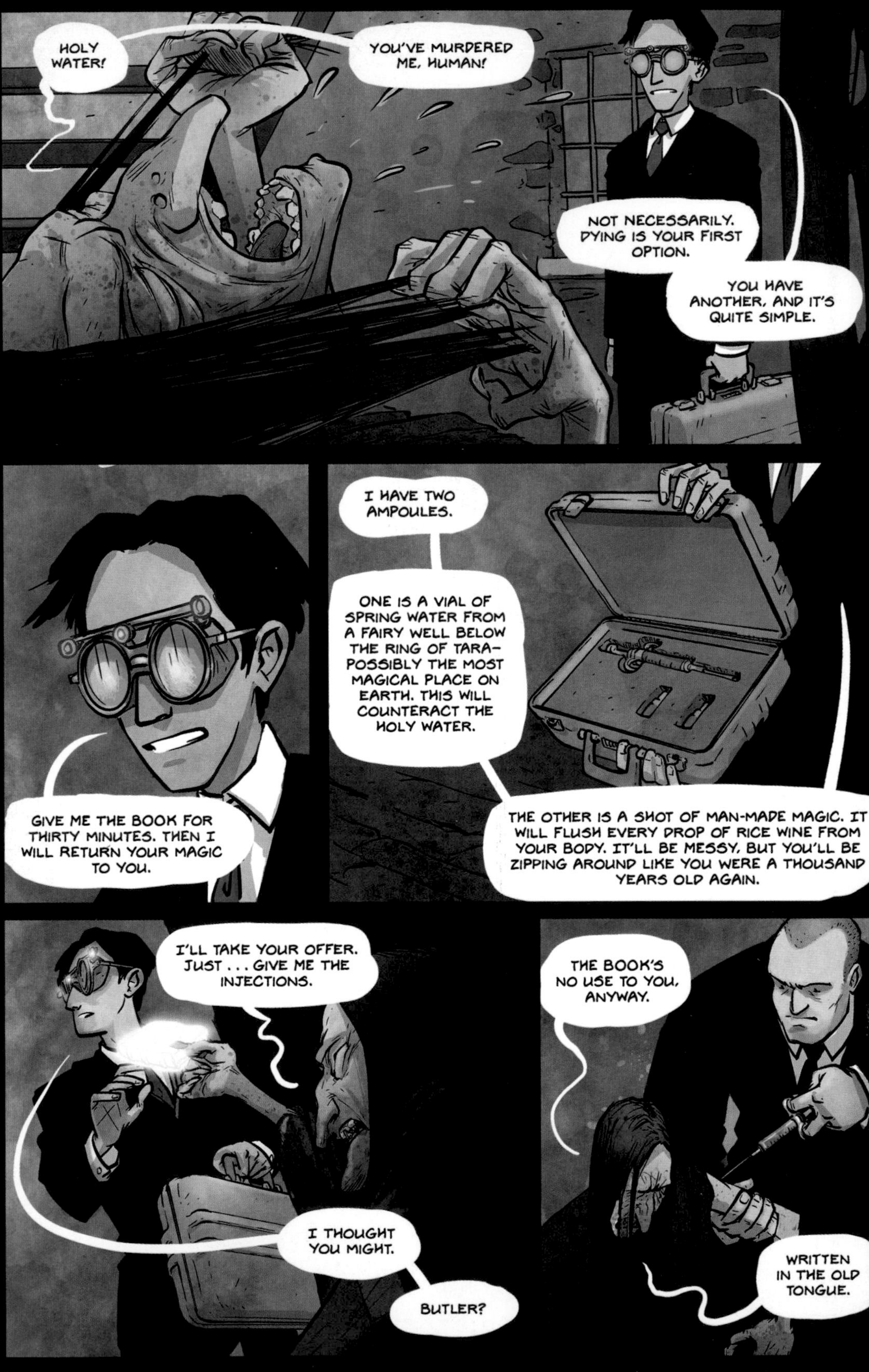
HOLY WATER!
YOU'VE MURDERED ME, HUMAN!
NOT NECESSARILY. DYING IS YOUR FIRST OPTION.
YOU HAVE ANOTHER, AND IT'S QUITE SIMPLE.
GIVE ME THE BOOK FOR THIRTY MINUTES. THEN I WILL RETURN YOUR MAGIC TO YOU.
I HAVE TWO AMPOULES.
ONE IS A VIAL OF SPRING WATER FROM A FAIRY WELL BELOW THE RING OF TARA-POSSIBLY THE MOST MAGICAL PLACE ON EARTH. THIS WILL COUNTERACT THE HOLY WATER.
THE OTHER IS A SHOT OF MAN-MADE MAGIC. IT WILL FLUSH EVERY DROP OF RICE WINE FROM YOUR BODY. IT'LL BE MESSY, BUT YOU'LL BE ZIPPING AROUND LIKE YOU WERE A THOUSAND YEARS OLD AGAIN.
I'LL TAKE YOUR OFFER. JUST . . . GIVE ME THE INJECTIONS.
I THOUGHT YOU MIGHT.
BUTLER?
THE BOOK'S NO USE TO YOU, ANYWAY.
WRITTEN IN THE OLD TONGUE.

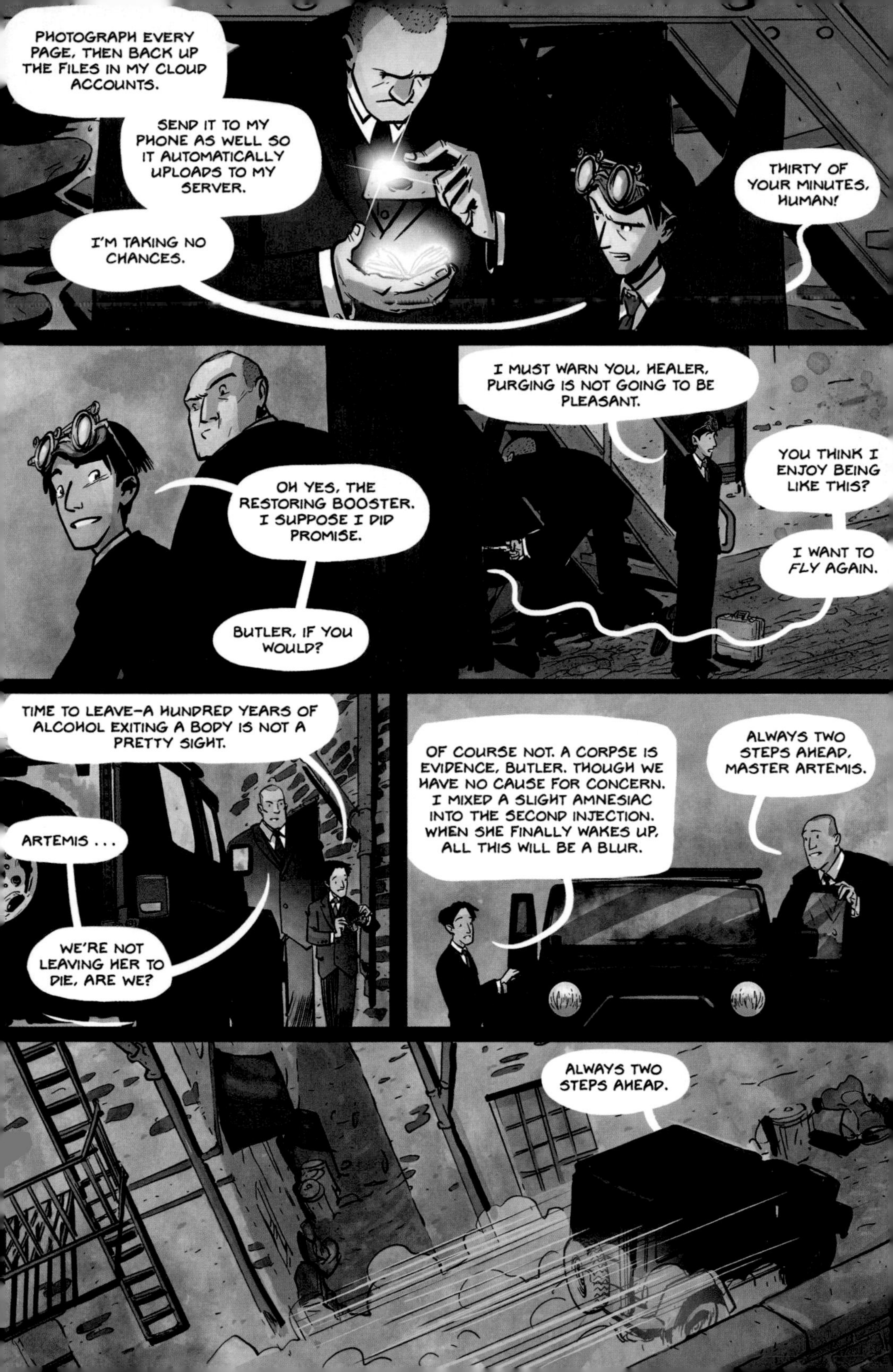
PHOTOGRAPH EVERY PAGE, THEN BACK UP THE FILES IN MY CLOUD ACCOUNTS.
SEND IT TO MY PHONE AS WELL SO IT AUTOMATICALLY UPLOADS TO MY SERVER.
I'M TAKING NO CHANCES.
THIRTY OF YOUR MINUTES, HUMAN!
OH YES, THE RESTORING BOOSTER. I SUPPOSE I DID PROMISE.
BUTLER, IF YOU WOULD?
I MUST WARN YOU, HEALER, PURGING IS NOT GOING TO BE PLEASANT.
YOU THINK I ENJOY BEING LIKE THIS?
I WANT TO *FLY* AGAIN.
TIME TO LEAVE—A HUNDRED YEARS OF ALCOHOL EXITING A BODY IS NOT A PRETTY SIGHT.
ARTEMIS . . .
WE'RE NOT LEAVING HER TO DIE, ARE WE?
OF COURSE NOT. A CORPSE IS EVIDENCE, BUTLER. THOUGH WE HAVE NO CAUSE FOR CONCERN. I MIXED A SLIGHT AMNESIAC INTO THE SECOND INJECTION. WHEN SHE FINALLY WAKES UP, ALL THIS WILL BE A BLUR.
ALWAYS TWO STEPS AHEAD, MASTER ARTEMIS.
ALWAYS TWO STEPS AHEAD.

CHAPTER TWO

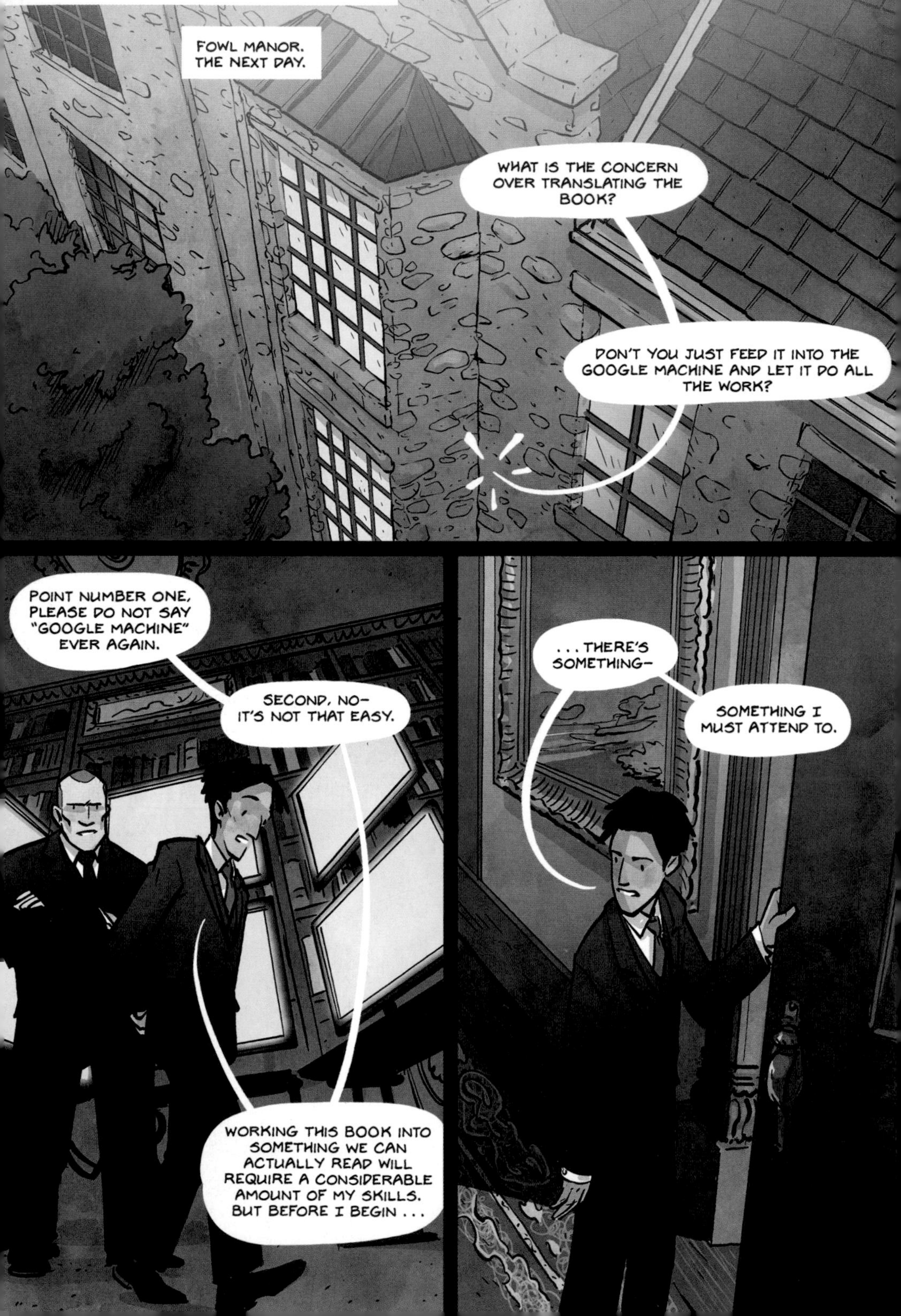
FOWL MANOR.
THE NEXT DAY.
WHAT IS THE CONCERN OVER TRANSLATING THE BOOK?
DON'T YOU JUST FEED IT INTO THE GOOGLE MACHINE AND LET IT DO ALL THE WORK?
POINT NUMBER ONE, PLEASE DO NOT SAY "GOOGLE MACHINE" EVER AGAIN.
SECOND, NO– IT'S NOT THAT EASY.
WORKING THIS BOOK INTO SOMETHING WE CAN ACTUALLY READ WILL REQUIRE A CONSIDERABLE AMOUNT OF MY SKILLS. BUT BEFORE I BEGIN . . .
. . . THERE'S SOMETHING–
SOMETHING I MUST ATTEND TO.

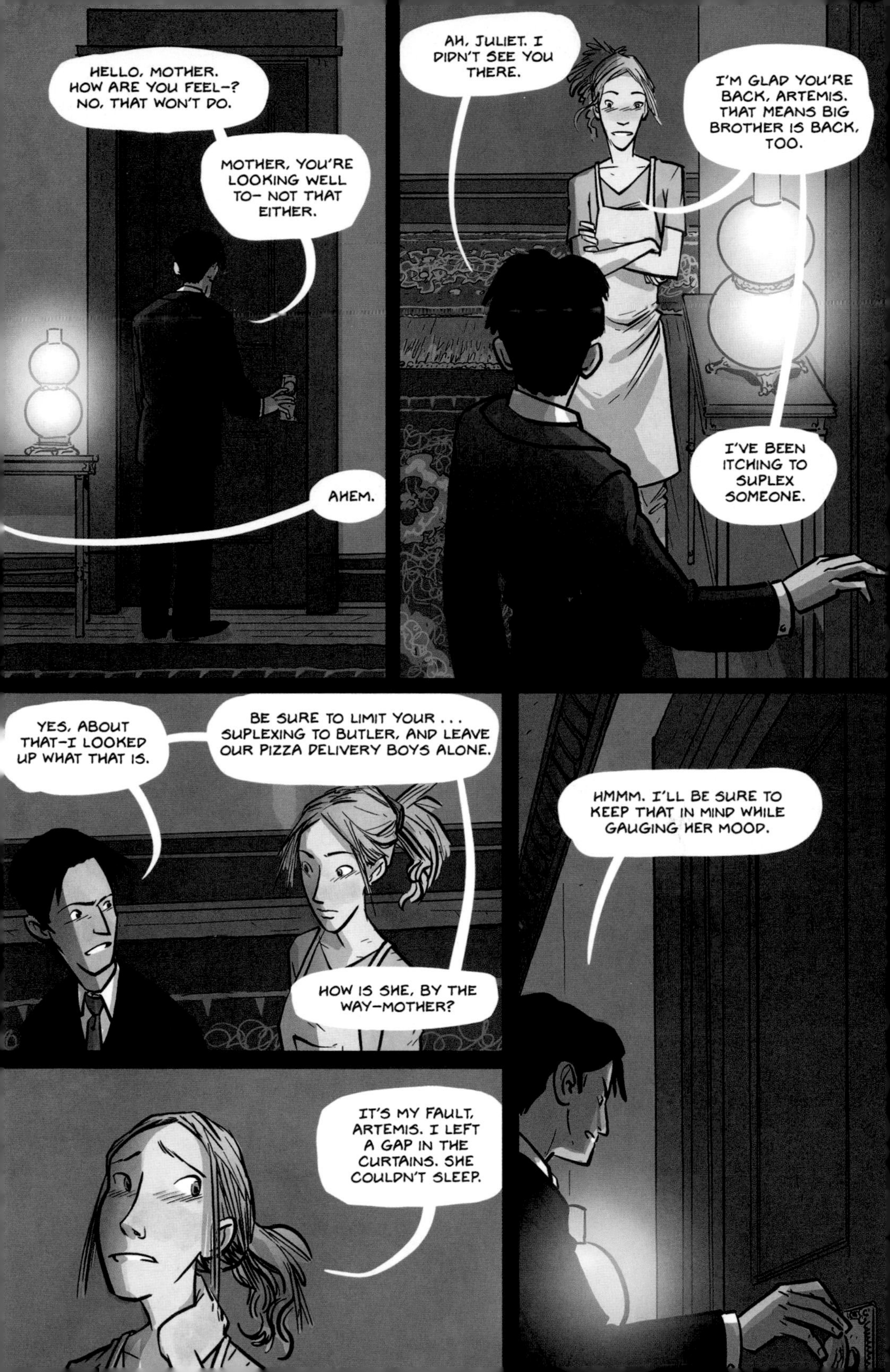
HELLO, MOTHER. HOW ARE YOU FEEL–? NO, THAT WON'T DO.
MOTHER, YOU'RE LOOKING WELL TO– NOT THAT EITHER.
AHEM.
AH, JULIET. I DIDN'T SEE YOU THERE.
I'M GLAD YOU'RE BACK, ARTEMIS. THAT MEANS BIG BROTHER IS BACK, TOO.
I'VE BEEN ITCHING TO SUPLEX SOMEONE.
YES, ABOUT THAT–I LOOKED UP WHAT THAT IS.
BE SURE TO LIMIT YOUR . . . SUPLEXING TO BUTLER, AND LEAVE OUR PIZZA DELIVERY BOYS ALONE.
HOW IS SHE, BY THE WAY–MOTHER?
IT'S MY FAULT, ARTEMIS. I LEFT A GAP IN THE CURTAINS. SHE COULDN'T SLEEP.
HMMM. I'LL BE SURE TO KEEP THAT IN MIND WHILE GAUGING HER MOOD.

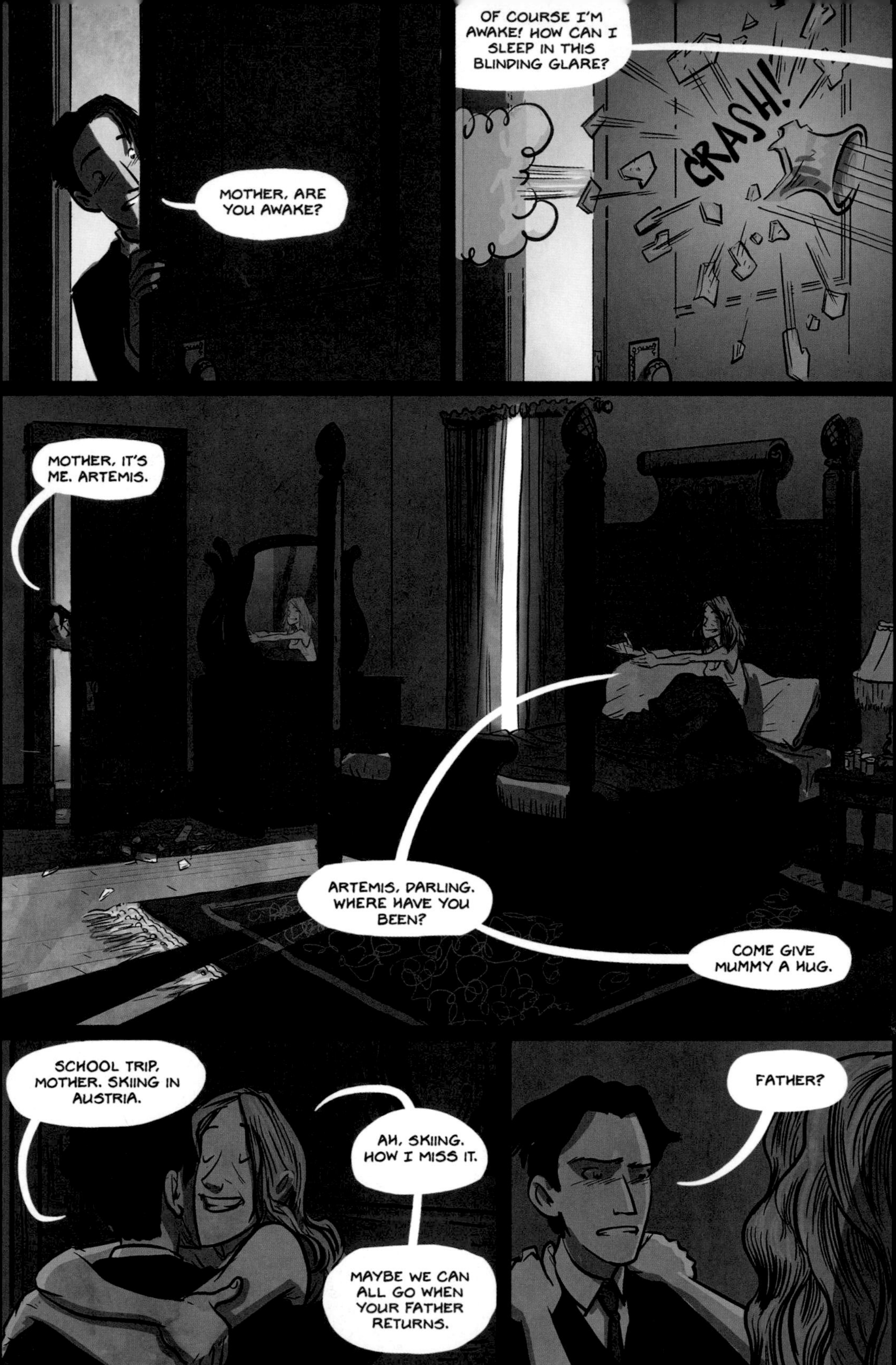
MOTHER, ARE YOU AWAKE?
OF COURSE I'M AWAKE! HOW CAN I SLEEP IN THIS BLINDING GLARE?
CRASH!
MOTHER, IT'S ME. ARTEMIS.
ARTEMIS, DARLING. WHERE HAVE YOU BEEN?
COME GIVE MUMMY A HUG.
SCHOOL TRIP, MOTHER. SKIING IN AUSTRIA.
AH, SKIING. HOW I MISS IT.
MAYBE WE CAN ALL GO WHEN YOUR FATHER RETURNS.
FATHER?

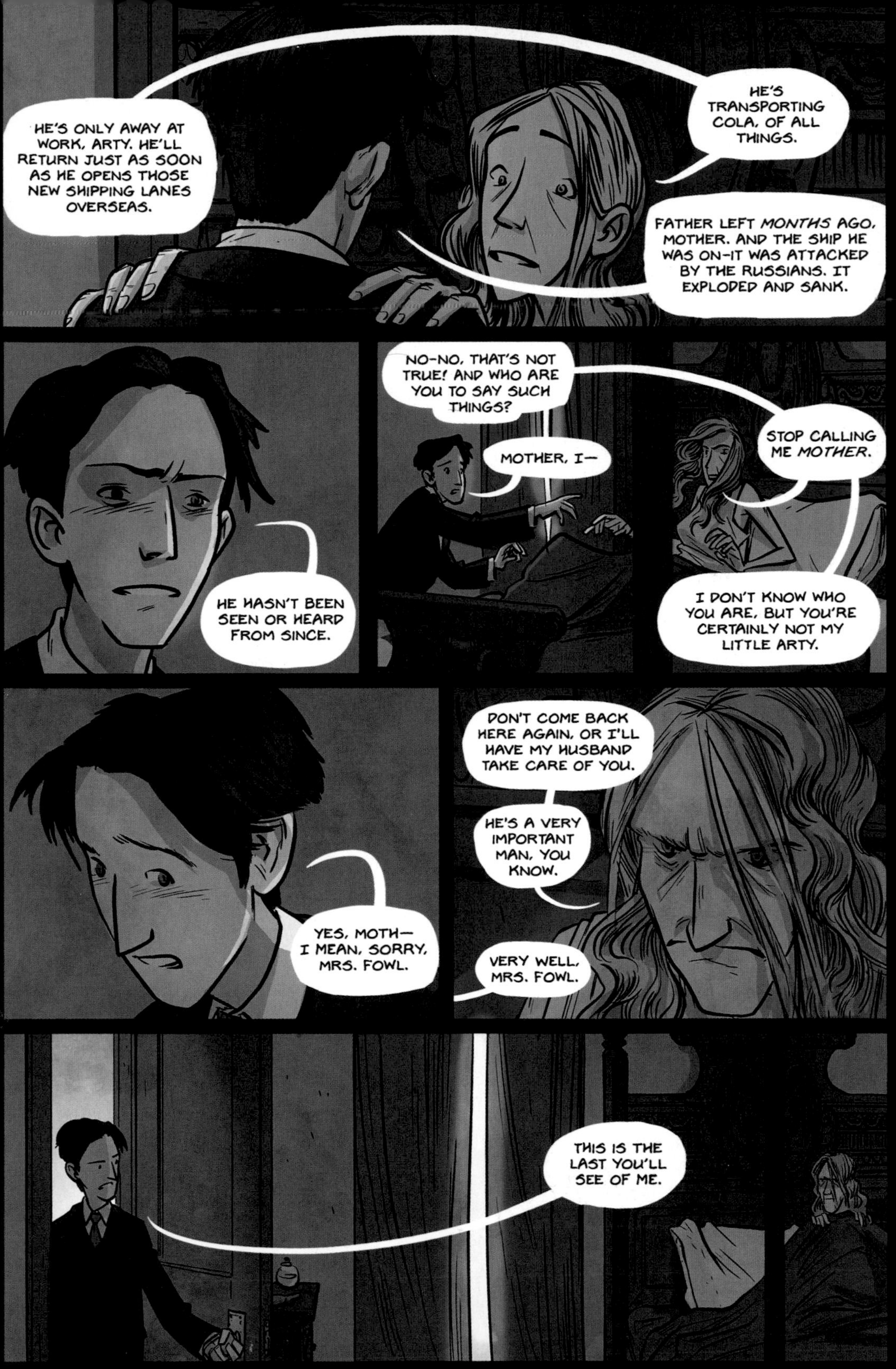
HE'S ONLY AWAY AT WORK, ARTY. HE'LL RETURN JUST AS SOON AS HE OPENS THOSE NEW SHIPPING LANES OVERSEAS.
HE'S TRANSPORTING COLA, OF ALL THINGS.
FATHER LEFT *MONTHS* AGO, MOTHER. AND THE SHIP HE WAS ON—IT WAS ATTACKED BY THE RUSSIANS. IT EXPLODED AND SANK.
HE HASN'T BEEN SEEN OR HEARD FROM SINCE.
NO-NO, THAT'S NOT TRUE! AND WHO ARE YOU TO SAY SUCH THINGS?
MOTHER, I—
STOP CALLING ME *MOTHER*.
I DON'T KNOW WHO YOU ARE, BUT YOU'RE CERTAINLY NOT MY LITTLE ARTY.
DON'T COME BACK HERE AGAIN, OR I'LL HAVE MY HUSBAND TAKE CARE OF YOU.
HE'S A VERY IMPORTANT MAN, YOU KNOW.
YES, MOTH— I MEAN, SORRY, MRS. FOWL.
VERY WELL, MRS. FOWL.
THIS IS THE LAST YOU'LL SEE OF ME.

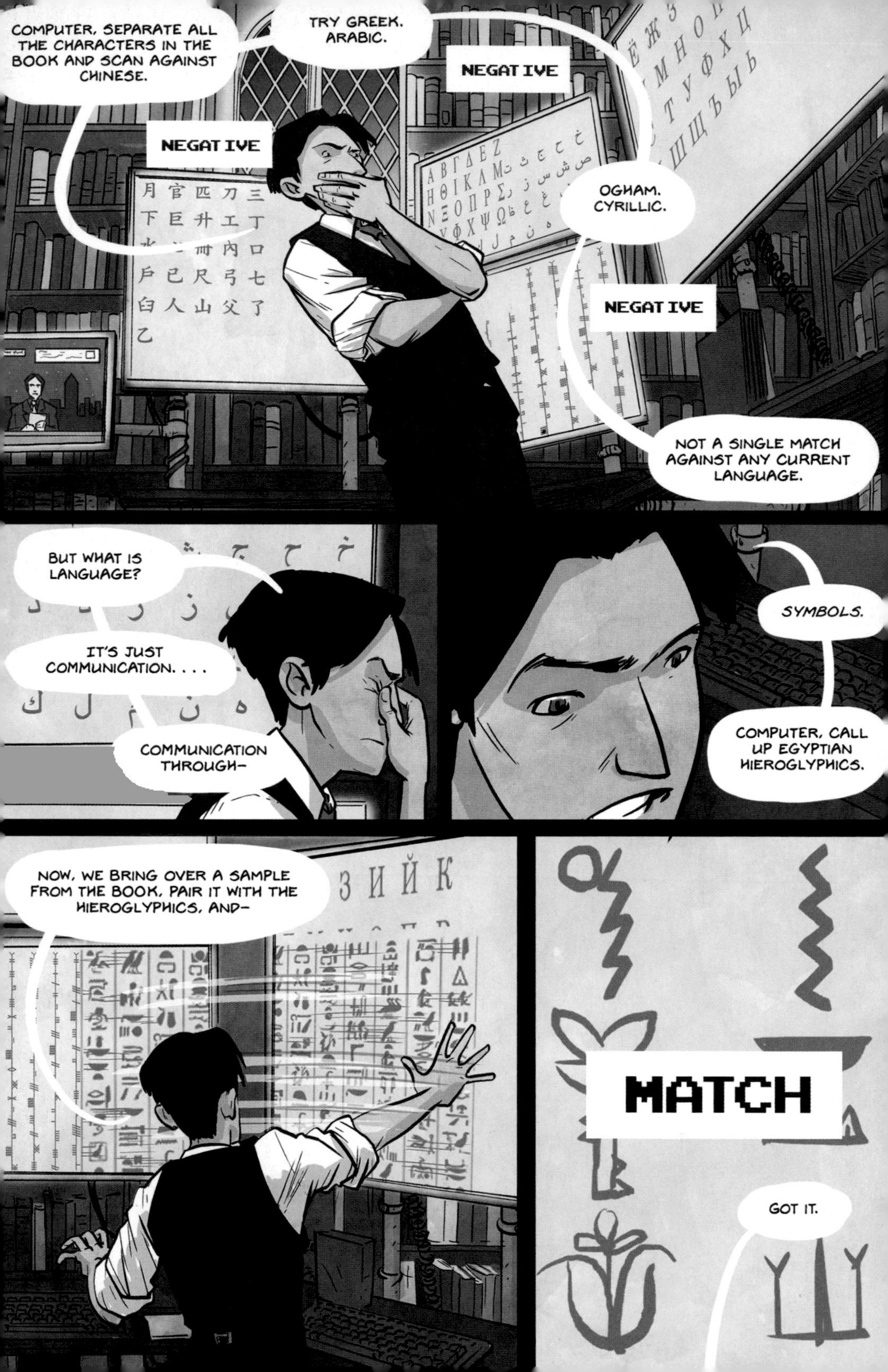
COMPUTER, SEPARATE ALL THE CHARACTERS IN THE BOOK AND SCAN AGAINST CHINESE.
NEGATIVE
TRY GREEK. ARABIC.
NEGATIVE
OGHAM. CYRILLIC.
NEGATIVE
NOT A SINGLE MATCH AGAINST ANY CURRENT LANGUAGE.
BUT WHAT IS LANGUAGE?
IT'S JUST COMMUNICATION. . . .
COMMUNICATION THROUGH–
SYMBOLS.
COMPUTER, CALL UP EGYPTIAN HIEROGLYPHICS.
NOW, WE BRING OVER A SAMPLE FROM THE BOOK, PAIR IT WITH THE HIEROGLYPHICS, AND–
MATCH
GOT IT.

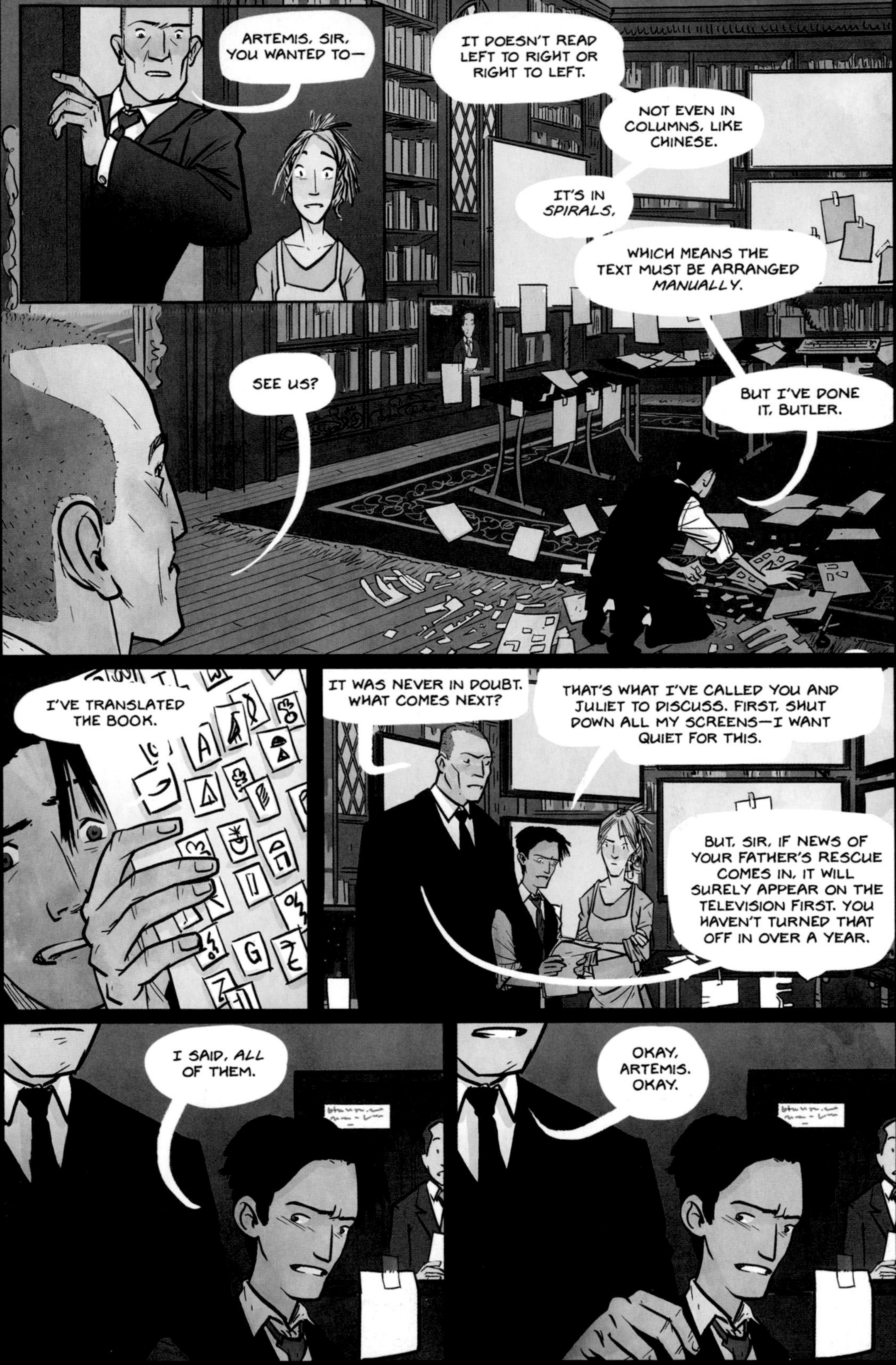
ARTEMIS, SIR, YOU WANTED TO—
IT DOESN'T READ LEFT TO RIGHT OR RIGHT TO LEFT.
NOT EVEN IN COLUMNS, LIKE CHINESE.
IT'S IN SPIRALS,
WHICH MEANS THE TEXT MUST BE ARRANGED MANUALLY.
SEE US?
BUT I'VE DONE IT, BUTLER.
I'VE TRANSLATED THE BOOK.
IT WAS NEVER IN DOUBT. WHAT COMES NEXT?
THAT'S WHAT I'VE CALLED YOU AND JULIET TO DISCUSS. FIRST, SHUT DOWN ALL MY SCREENS—I WANT QUIET FOR THIS.
BUT, SIR, IF NEWS OF YOUR FATHER'S RESCUE COMES IN, IT WILL SURELY APPEAR ON THE TELEVISION FIRST. YOU HAVEN'T TURNED THAT OFF IN OVER A YEAR.
I SAID, ALL OF THEM.
OKAY, ARTEMIS. OKAY.

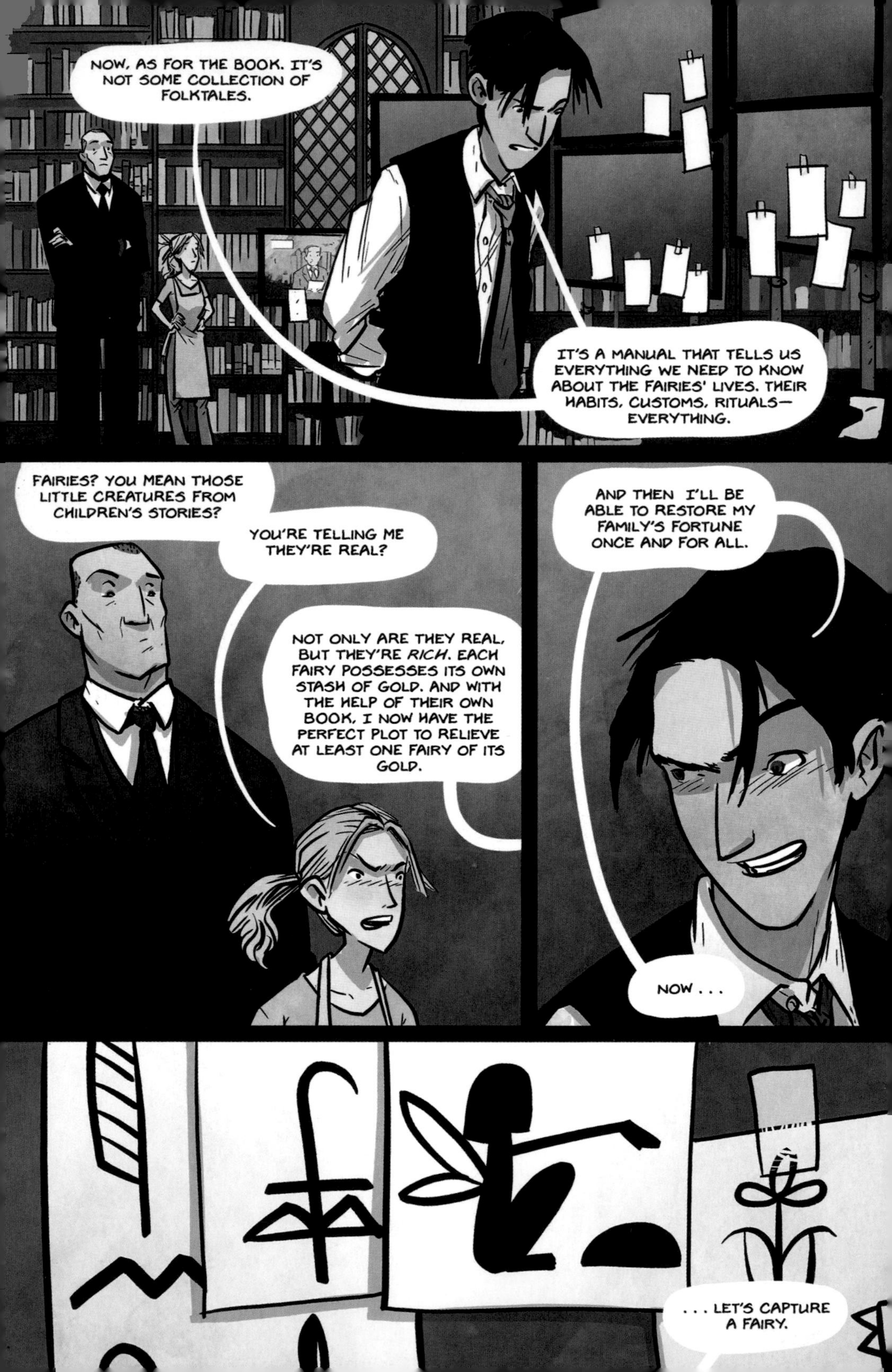
NOW, AS FOR THE BOOK. IT'S NOT SOME COLLECTION OF FOLKTALES.
IT'S A MANUAL THAT TELLS US EVERYTHING WE NEED TO KNOW ABOUT THE FAIRIES' LIVES. THEIR HABITS, CUSTOMS, RITUALS—EVERYTHING.
FAIRIES? YOU MEAN THOSE LITTLE CREATURES FROM CHILDREN'S STORIES?
YOU'RE TELLING ME THEY'RE REAL?
NOT ONLY ARE THEY REAL, BUT THEY'RE *RICH*. EACH FAIRY POSSESSES ITS OWN STASH OF GOLD. AND WITH THE HELP OF THEIR OWN BOOK, I NOW HAVE THE PERFECT PLOT TO RELIEVE AT LEAST ONE FAIRY OF ITS GOLD.
AND THEN I'LL BE ABLE TO RESTORE MY FAMILY'S FORTUNE ONCE AND FOR ALL.
NOW . . .
. . . LET'S CAPTURE A FAIRY.

CHAPTER THREE

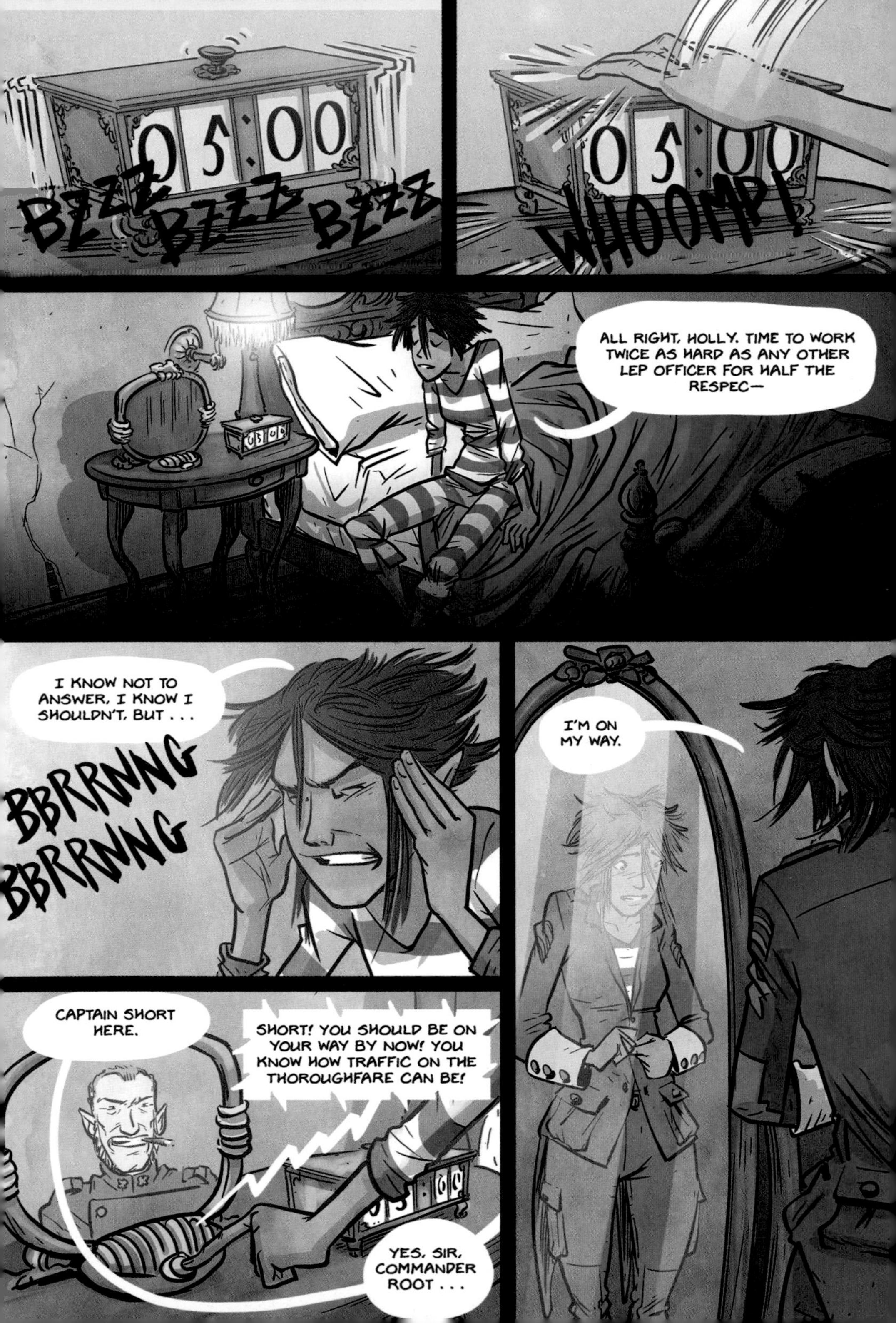
05:00
BZZZ BZZZ BZZZ
05:00
WHOOMP!
ALL RIGHT, HOLLY. TIME TO WORK TWICE AS HARD AS ANY OTHER LEP OFFICER FOR HALF THE RESPEC—
I KNOW NOT TO ANSWER, I KNOW I SHOULDN'T, BUT . . .
BBRRNNG
BBRRNNG
CAPTAIN SHORT HERE.
SHORT! YOU SHOULD BE ON YOUR WAY BY NOW! YOU KNOW HOW TRAFFIC ON THE THOROUGHFARE CAN BE!
YES, SIR, COMMANDER ROOT . . .
I'M ON MY WAY.

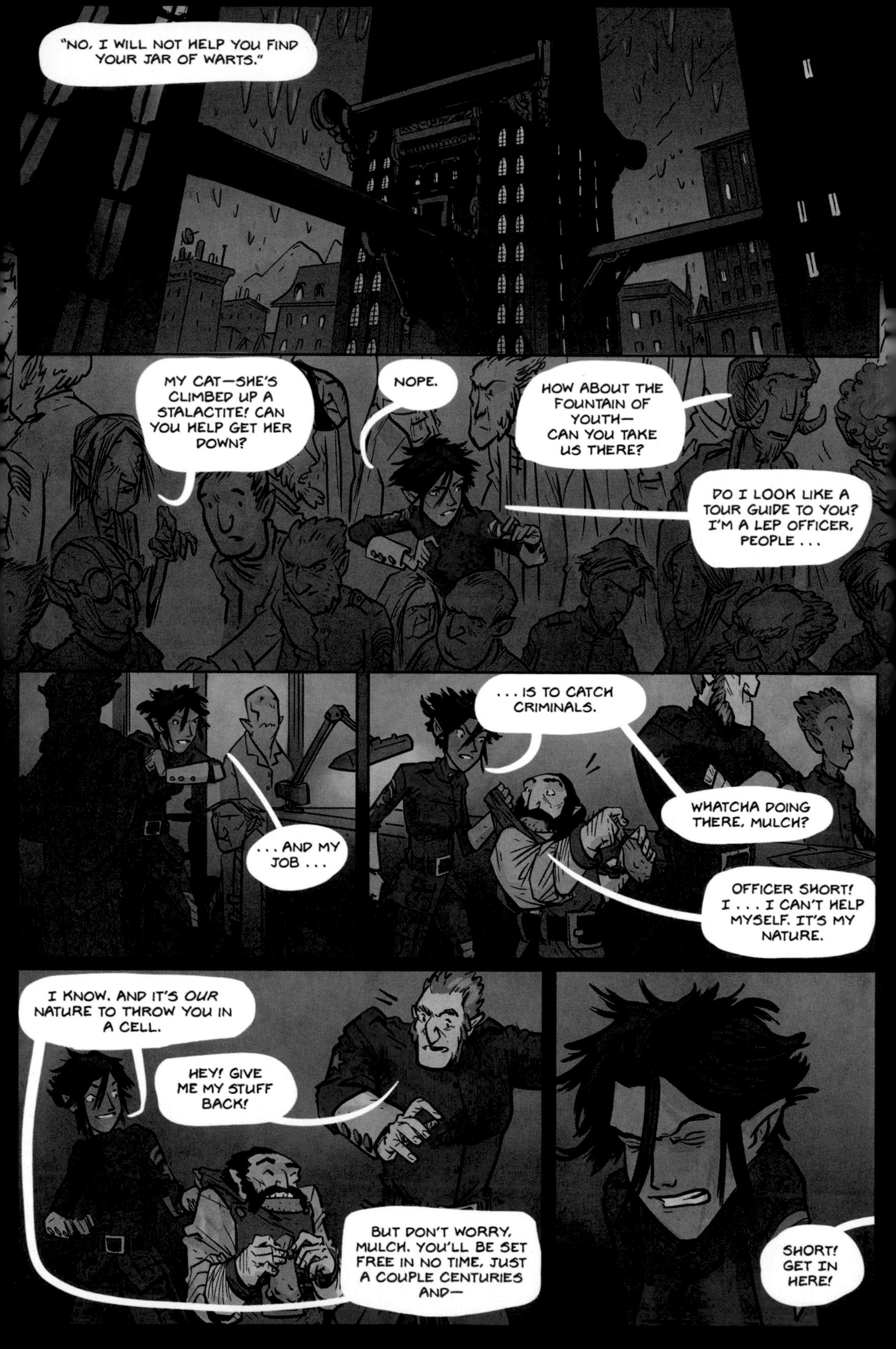
"NO, I WILL NOT HELP YOU FIND YOUR JAR OF WARTS."
MY CAT—SHE'S CLIMBED UP A STALACTITE! CAN YOU HELP GET HER DOWN?
NOPE.
HOW ABOUT THE FOUNTAIN OF YOUTH— CAN YOU TAKE US THERE?
DO I LOOK LIKE A TOUR GUIDE TO YOU? I'M A LEP OFFICER, PEOPLE . . .
. . . AND MY JOB . . .
. . . IS TO CATCH CRIMINALS.
WHATCHA DOING THERE, MULCH?
OFFICER SHORT! I . . . I CAN'T HELP MYSELF. IT'S MY NATURE.
I KNOW. AND IT'S *OUR* NATURE TO THROW YOU IN A CELL.
HEY! GIVE ME MY STUFF BACK!
BUT DON'T WORRY, MULCH. YOU'LL BE SET FREE IN NO TIME, JUST A COUPLE CENTURIES AND—
SHORT! GET IN HERE!

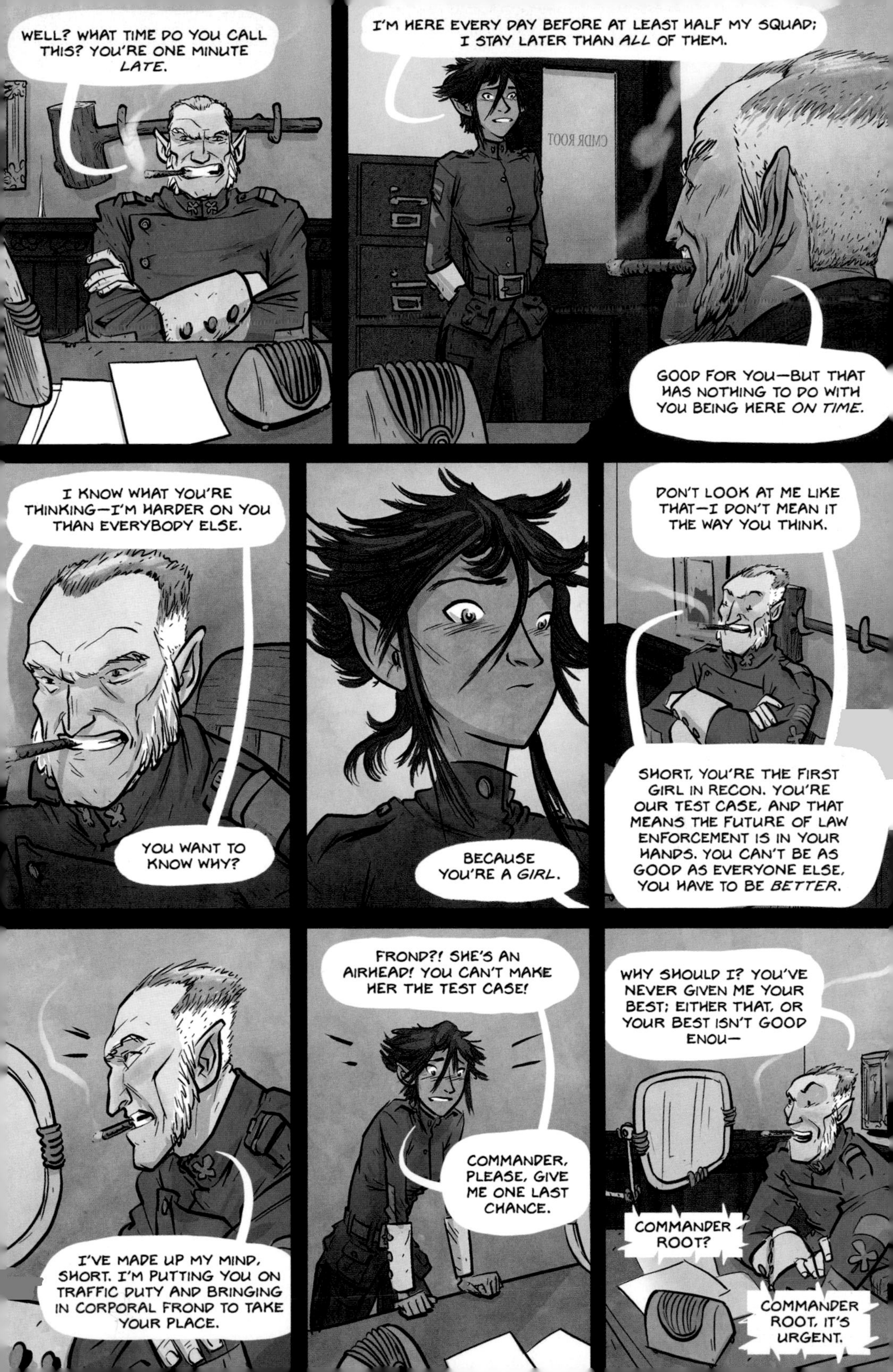

WELL? WHAT TIME DO YOU CALL THIS? YOU'RE ONE MINUTE *LATE*.
I'M HERE EVERY DAY BEFORE AT LEAST HALF MY SQUAD; I STAY LATER THAN *ALL* OF THEM.
GOOD FOR YOU—BUT THAT HAS NOTHING TO DO WITH YOU BEING HERE *ON TIME*.
I KNOW WHAT YOU'RE THINKING—I'M HARDER ON YOU THAN EVERYBODY ELSE.
YOU WANT TO KNOW WHY?
BECAUSE YOU'RE A *GIRL*.
DON'T LOOK AT ME LIKE THAT—I DON'T MEAN IT THE WAY YOU THINK.
SHORT, YOU'RE THE FIRST GIRL IN RECON. YOU'RE OUR TEST CASE, AND THAT MEANS THE FUTURE OF LAW ENFORCEMENT IS IN YOUR HANDS. YOU CAN'T BE AS GOOD AS EVERYONE ELSE, YOU HAVE TO BE *BETTER*.
I'VE MADE UP MY MIND, SHORT. I'M PUTTING YOU ON TRAFFIC DUTY AND BRINGING IN CORPORAL FROND TO TAKE YOUR PLACE.
FROND?! SHE'S AN AIRHEAD! YOU CAN'T MAKE HER THE TEST CASE!
COMMANDER, PLEASE, GIVE ME ONE LAST CHANCE.
WHY SHOULD I? YOU'VE NEVER GIVEN ME YOUR BEST; EITHER THAT, OR YOUR BEST ISN'T GOOD ENOU—
COMMANDER ROOT?
COMMANDER ROOT, IT'S URGENT.

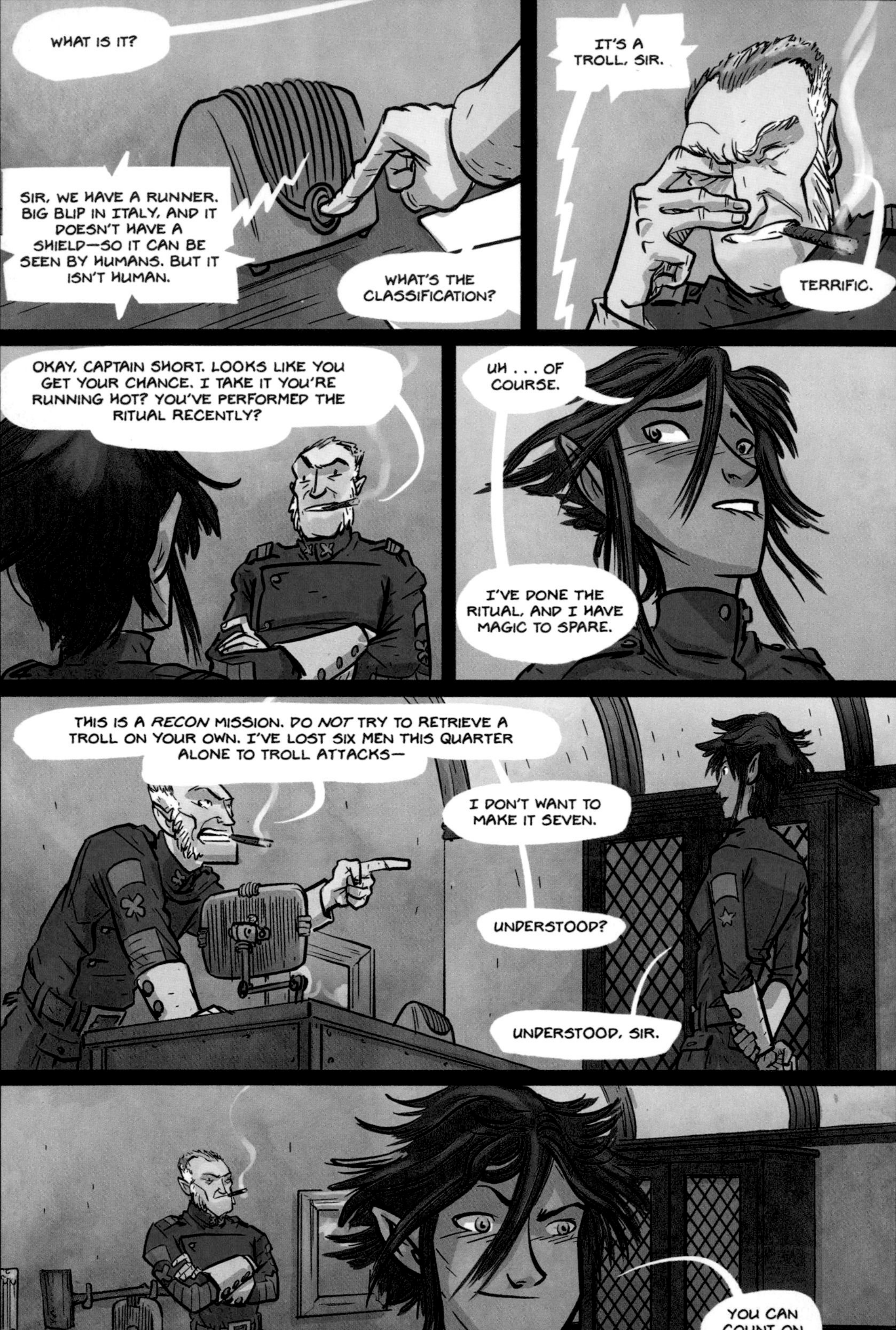
WHAT IS IT?
SIR, WE HAVE A RUNNER. BIG BLIP IN ITALY, AND IT DOESN'T HAVE A SHIELD—SO IT CAN BE SEEN BY HUMANS. BUT IT ISN'T HUMAN.
WHAT'S THE CLASSIFICATION?
IT'S A TROLL, SIR.
TERRIFIC.
OKAY, CAPTAIN SHORT. LOOKS LIKE YOU GET YOUR CHANCE. I TAKE IT YOU'RE RUNNING HOT? YOU'VE PERFORMED THE RITUAL RECENTLY?
UH . . . OF COURSE.
I'VE DONE THE RITUAL, AND I HAVE MAGIC TO SPARE.
THIS IS A *RECON* MISSION. DO *NOT* TRY TO RETRIEVE A TROLL ON YOUR OWN. I'VE LOST SIX MEN THIS QUARTER ALONE TO TROLL ATTACKS—
I DON'T WANT TO MAKE IT SEVEN.
UNDERSTOOD?
UNDERSTOOD, SIR.
YOU CAN COUNT ON ME.

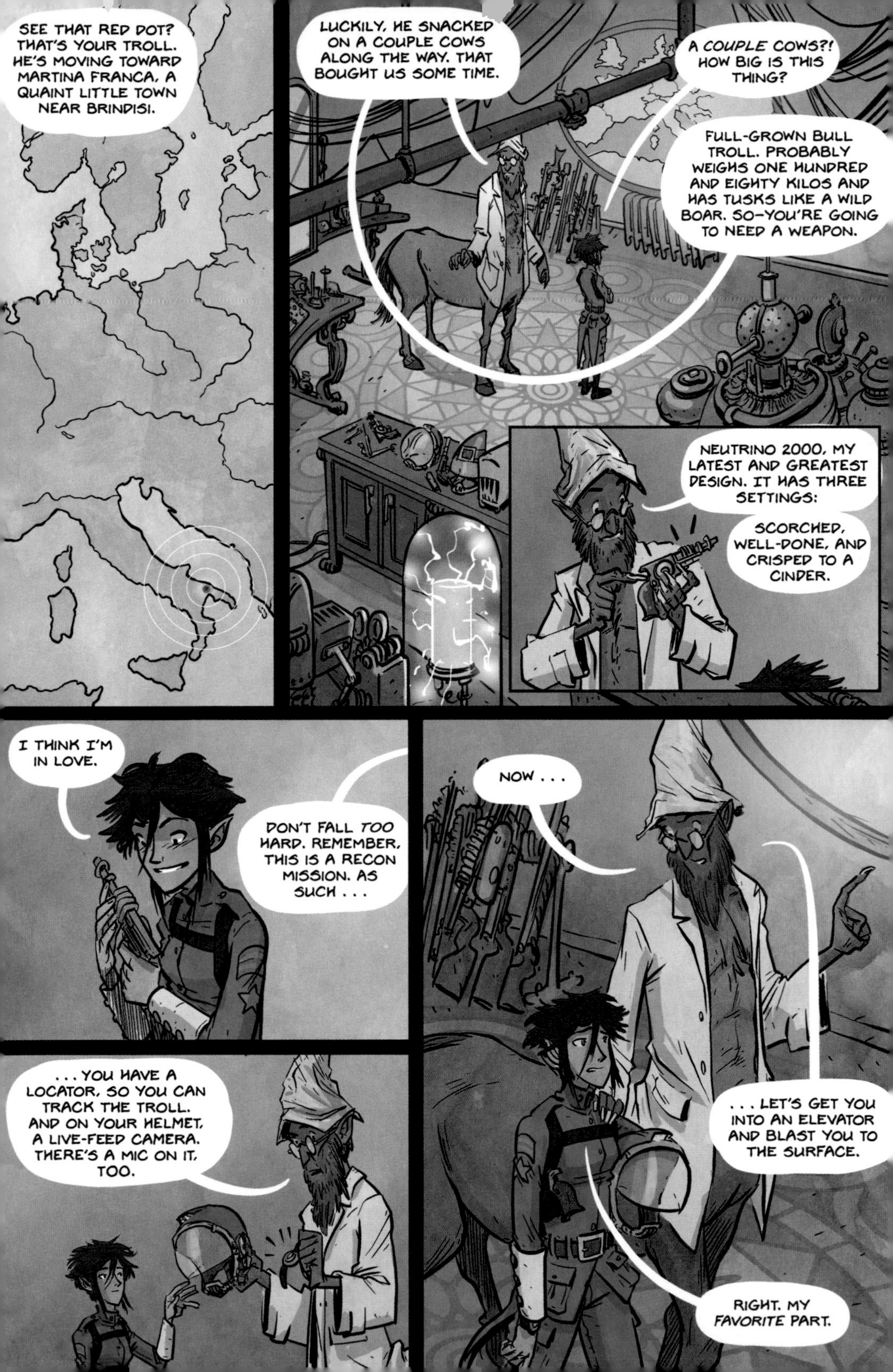
SEE THAT RED DOT? THAT'S YOUR TROLL. HE'S MOVING TOWARD MARTINA FRANCA, A QUAINT LITTLE TOWN NEAR BRINDISI.
LUCKILY, HE SNACKED ON A COUPLE COWS ALONG THE WAY. THAT BOUGHT US SOME TIME.
A *COUPLE* COWS?! HOW BIG IS THIS THING?
FULL-GROWN BULL TROLL. PROBABLY WEIGHS ONE HUNDRED AND EIGHTY KILOS AND HAS TUSKS LIKE A WILD BOAR. SO—YOU'RE GOING TO NEED A WEAPON.
NEUTRINO 2000, MY LATEST AND GREATEST DESIGN. IT HAS THREE SETTINGS:
SCORCHED, WELL-DONE, AND CRISPED TO A CINDER.
I THINK I'M IN LOVE.
DON'T FALL *TOO* HARD. REMEMBER, THIS IS A RECON MISSION. AS SUCH . . .
. . . YOU HAVE A LOCATOR, SO YOU CAN TRACK THE TROLL. AND ON YOUR HELMET, A LIVE-FEED CAMERA. THERE'S A MIC ON IT, TOO.
NOW . . .
. . . LET'S GET YOU INTO AN ELEVATOR AND BLAST YOU TO THE SURFACE.
RIGHT. MY *FAVORITE* PART.

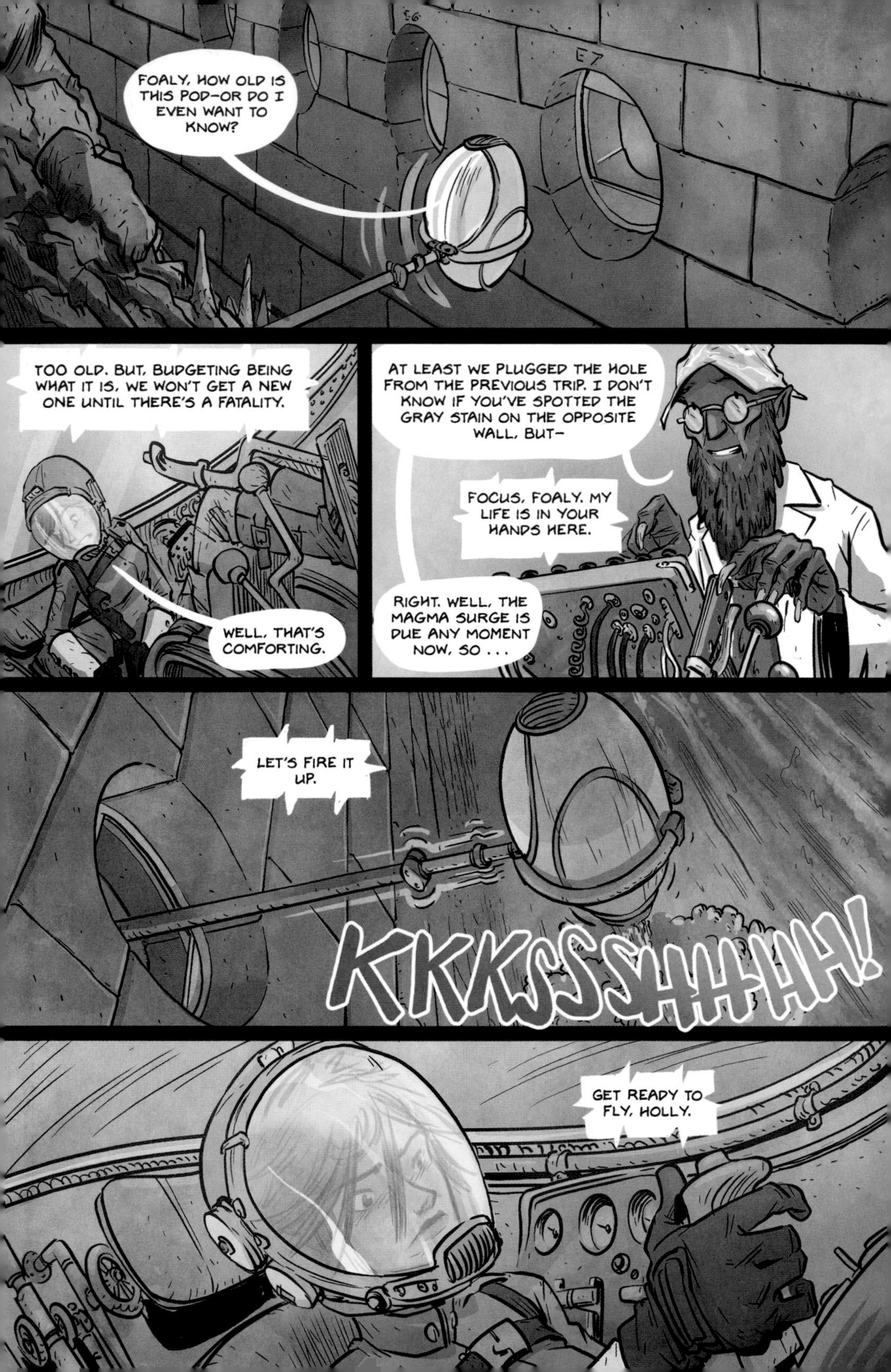
FOALY, HOW OLD IS THIS POD—OR DO I EVEN WANT TO KNOW?
TOO OLD. BUT, BUDGETING BEING WHAT IT IS, WE WON'T GET A NEW ONE UNTIL THERE'S A FATALITY.
WELL, THAT'S COMFORTING.
AT LEAST WE PLUGGED THE HOLE FROM THE PREVIOUS TRIP. I DON'T KNOW IF YOU'VE SPOTTED THE GRAY STAIN ON THE OPPOSITE WALL, BUT–
FOCUS, FOALY. MY LIFE IS IN YOUR HANDS HERE.
RIGHT. WELL, THE MAGMA SURGE IS DUE ANY MOMENT NOW, SO . . .
LET'S FIRE IT UP.
KKKSSHHHH!
GET READY TO FLY, HOLLY.

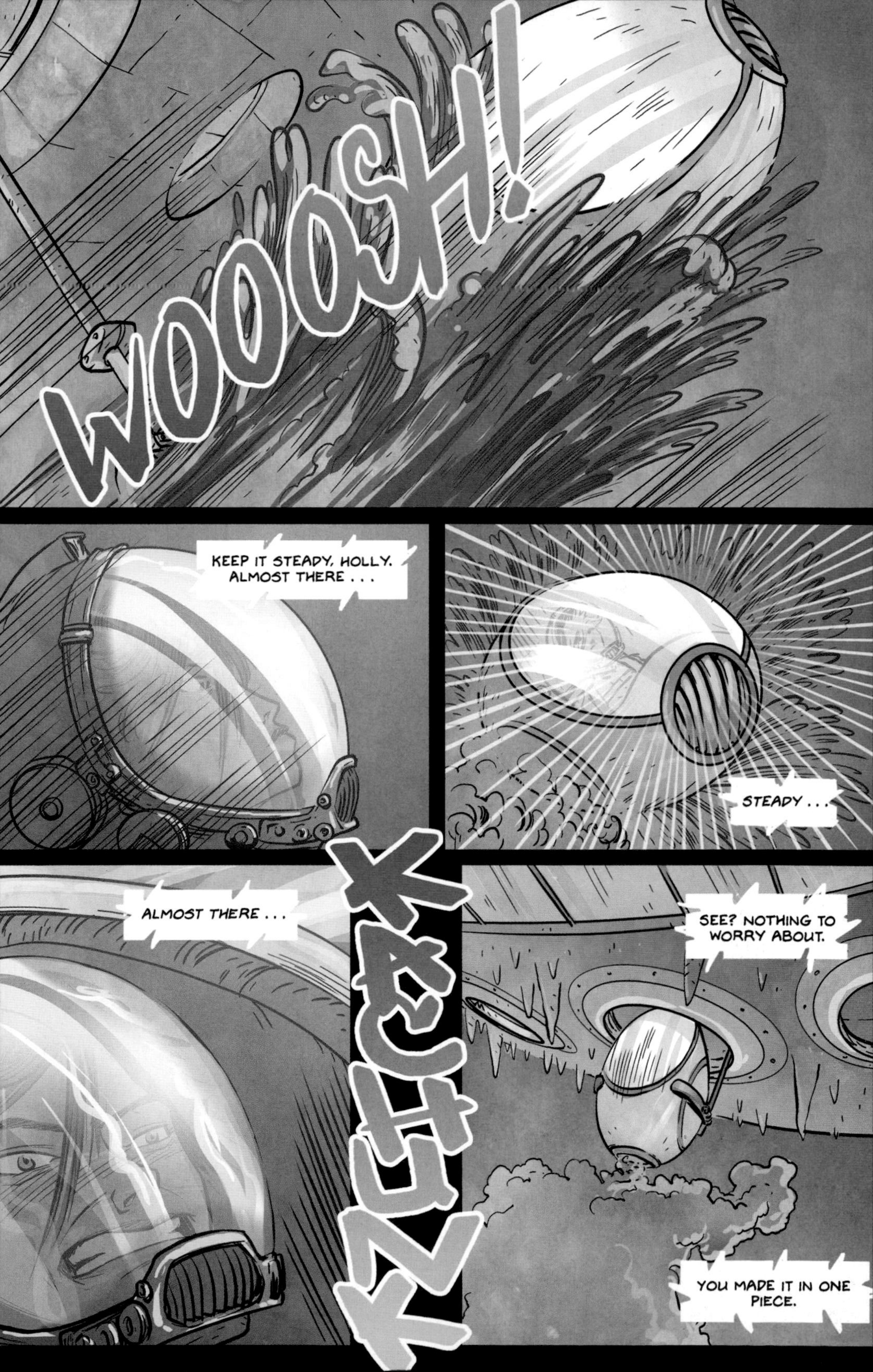
WOOOSH!
KEEP IT STEADY, HOLLY. ALMOST THERE . . .
STEADY . . .
ALMOST THERE . . .
KA-CHUNK
SEE? NOTHING TO WORRY ABOUT.
YOU MADE IT IN ONE PIECE.

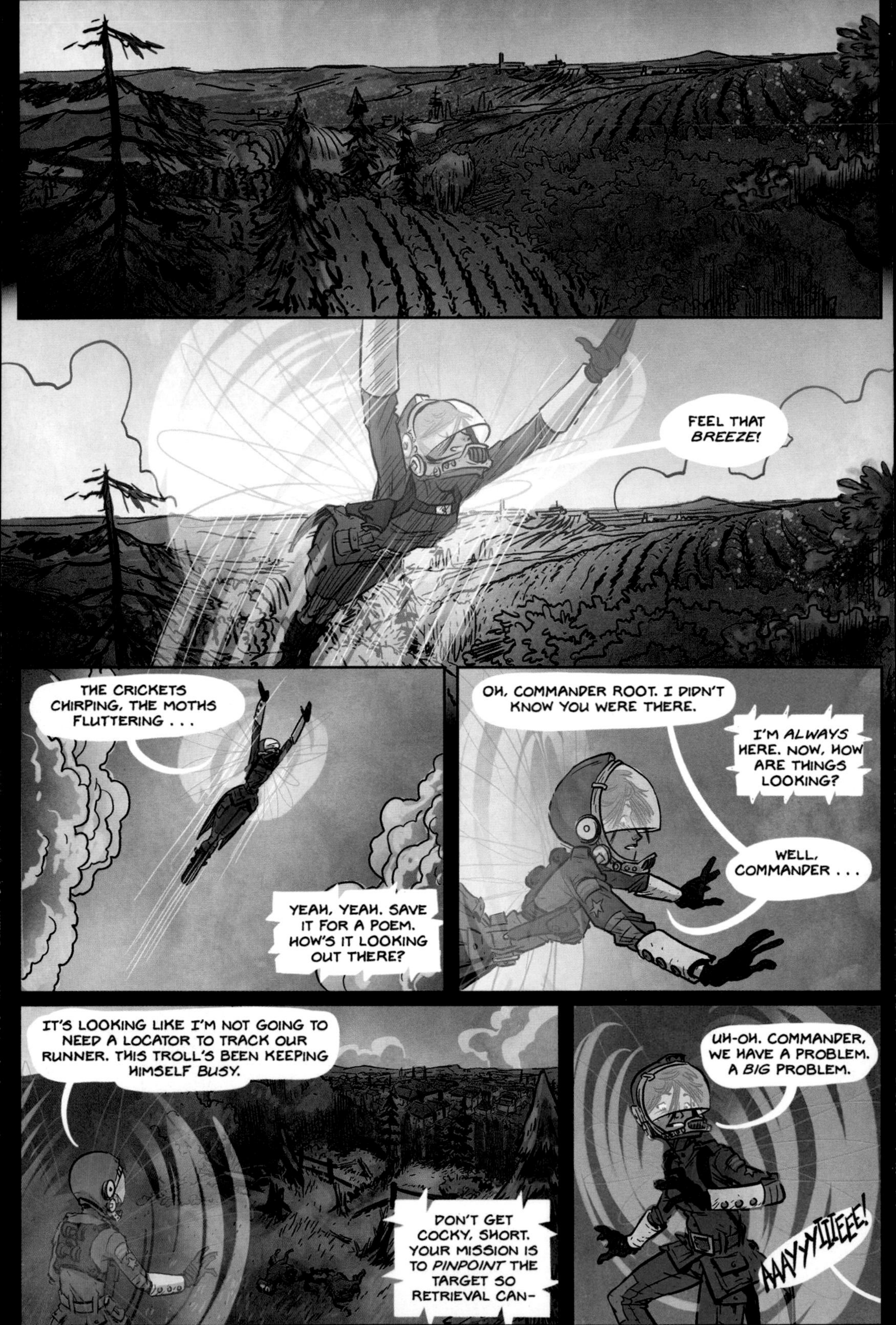
FEEL THAT *BREEZE!*
THE CRICKETS CHIRPING, THE MOTHS FLUTTERING . . .
YEAH, YEAH. SAVE IT FOR A POEM. HOW'S IT LOOKING OUT THERE?
OH, COMMANDER ROOT. I DIDN'T KNOW YOU WERE THERE.
I'M *ALWAYS* HERE. NOW, HOW ARE THINGS LOOKING?
WELL, COMMANDER . . .
IT'S LOOKING LIKE I'M NOT GOING TO NEED A LOCATOR TO TRACK OUR RUNNER. THIS TROLL'S BEEN KEEPING HIMSELF *BUSY.*
DON'T GET COCKY, SHORT. YOUR MISSION IS TO *PINPOINT* THE TARGET SO RETRIEVAL CAN–
UH-OH. COMMANDER, WE HAVE A PROBLEM. A *BIG* PROBLEM.
AAAYYYIIIEEE!

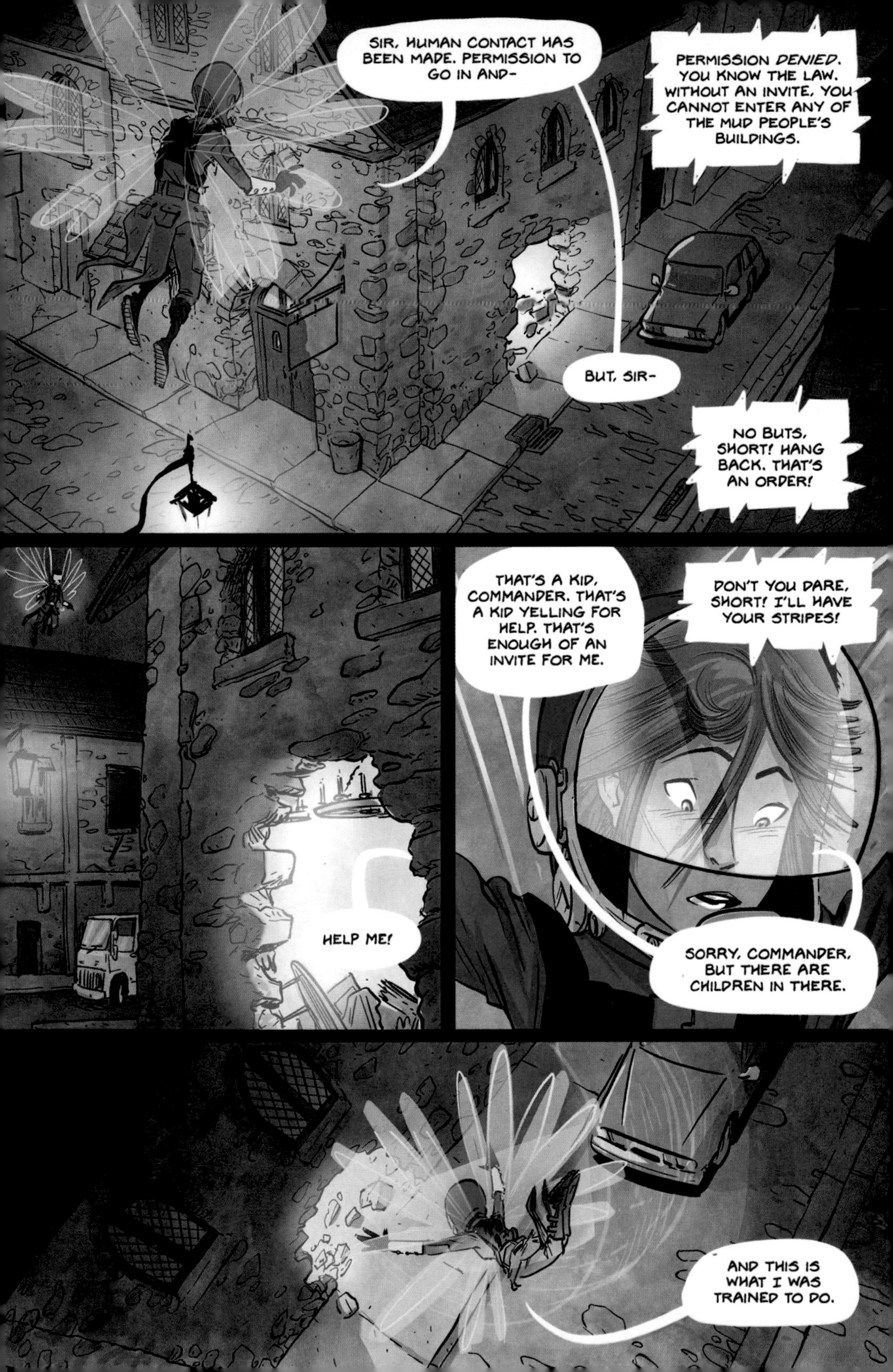
SIR, HUMAN CONTACT HAS BEEN MADE. PERMISSION TO GO IN AND-
PERMISSION *DENIED*. YOU KNOW THE LAW. WITHOUT AN INVITE, YOU CANNOT ENTER ANY OF THE MUD PEOPLE'S BUILDINGS.
BUT, SIR-
NO BUTS, SHORT! HANG BACK. THAT'S AN ORDER!
HELP ME!
THAT'S A KID, COMMANDER. THAT'S A KID YELLING FOR HELP. THAT'S ENOUGH OF AN INVITE FOR ME.
DON'T YOU DARE, SHORT! I'LL HAVE YOUR STRIPES!
SORRY, COMMANDER, BUT THERE ARE CHILDREN IN THERE.
AND THIS IS WHAT I WAS TRAINED TO DO.

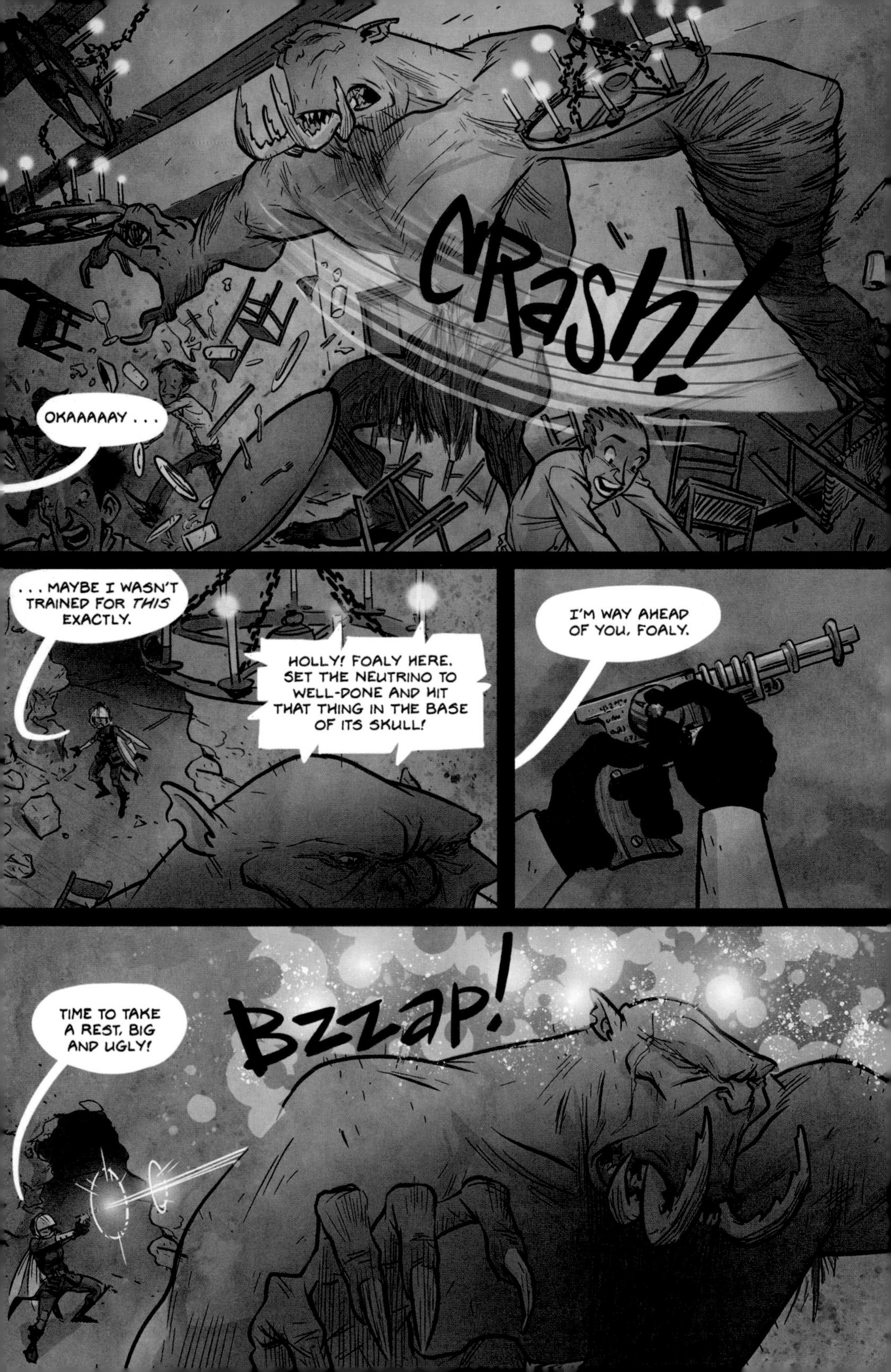
CRASH!
OKAAAAAY . . .
. . . MAYBE I WASN'T TRAINED FOR *THIS* EXACTLY.
HOLLY! FOALY HERE. SET THE NEUTRINO TO WELL-DONE AND HIT THAT THING IN THE BASE OF ITS SKULL!
I'M WAY AHEAD OF YOU, FOALY.
TIME TO TAKE A REST, BIG AND UGLY!
BZZAP!

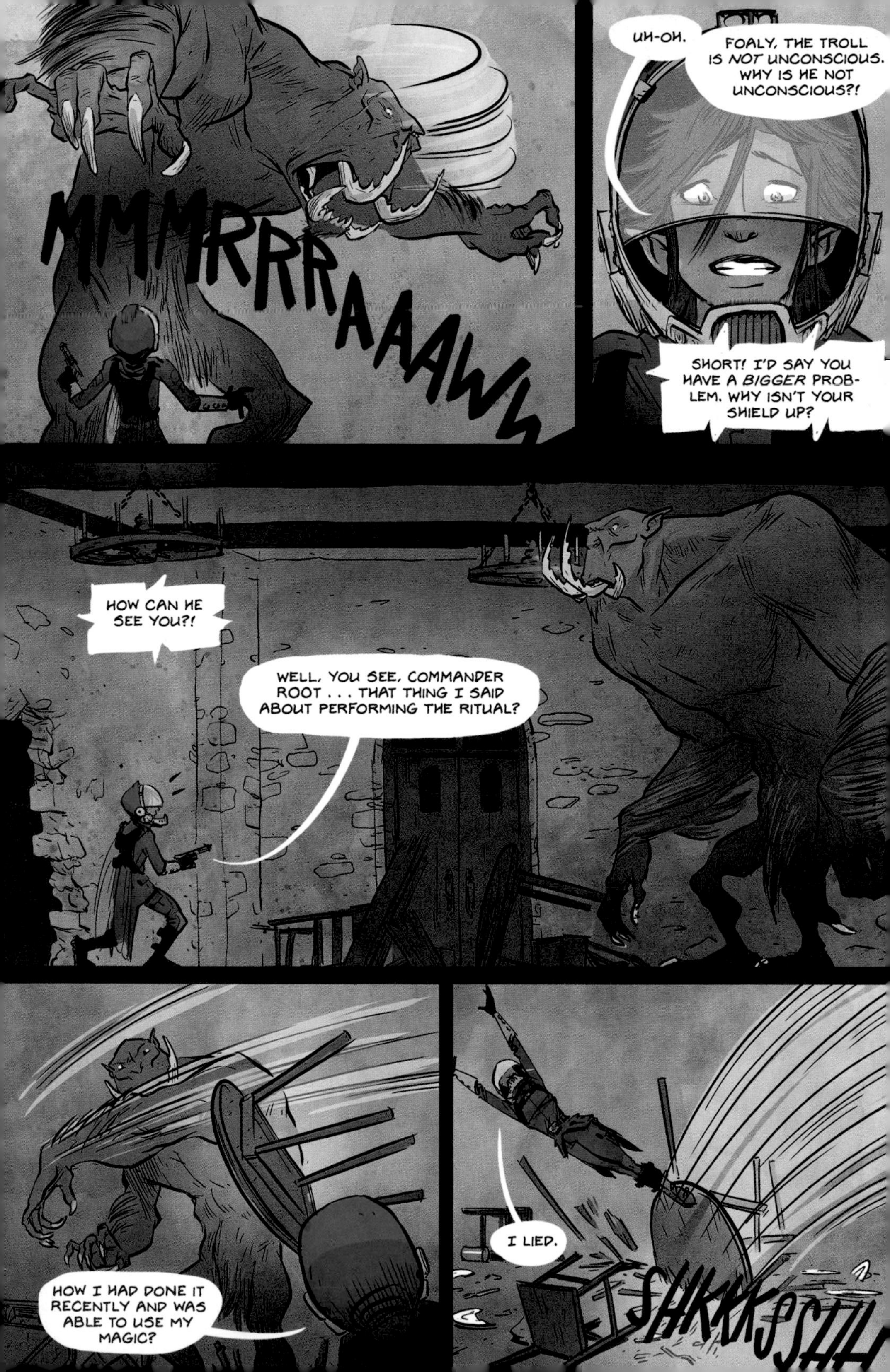
MMMRRRRAAAWW
UH-OH.
FOALY, THE TROLL IS *NOT* UNCONSCIOUS. WHY IS HE NOT UNCONSCIOUS?!
SHORT! I'D SAY YOU HAVE A *BIGGER* PROB-LEM. WHY ISN'T YOUR SHIELD UP?
HOW CAN HE SEE YOU?!
WELL, YOU SEE, COMMANDER ROOT . . . THAT THING I SAID ABOUT PERFORMING THE RITUAL?
HOW I HAD DONE IT RECENTLY AND WAS ABLE TO USE MY MAGIC?
I LIED.
SHKKKSHH

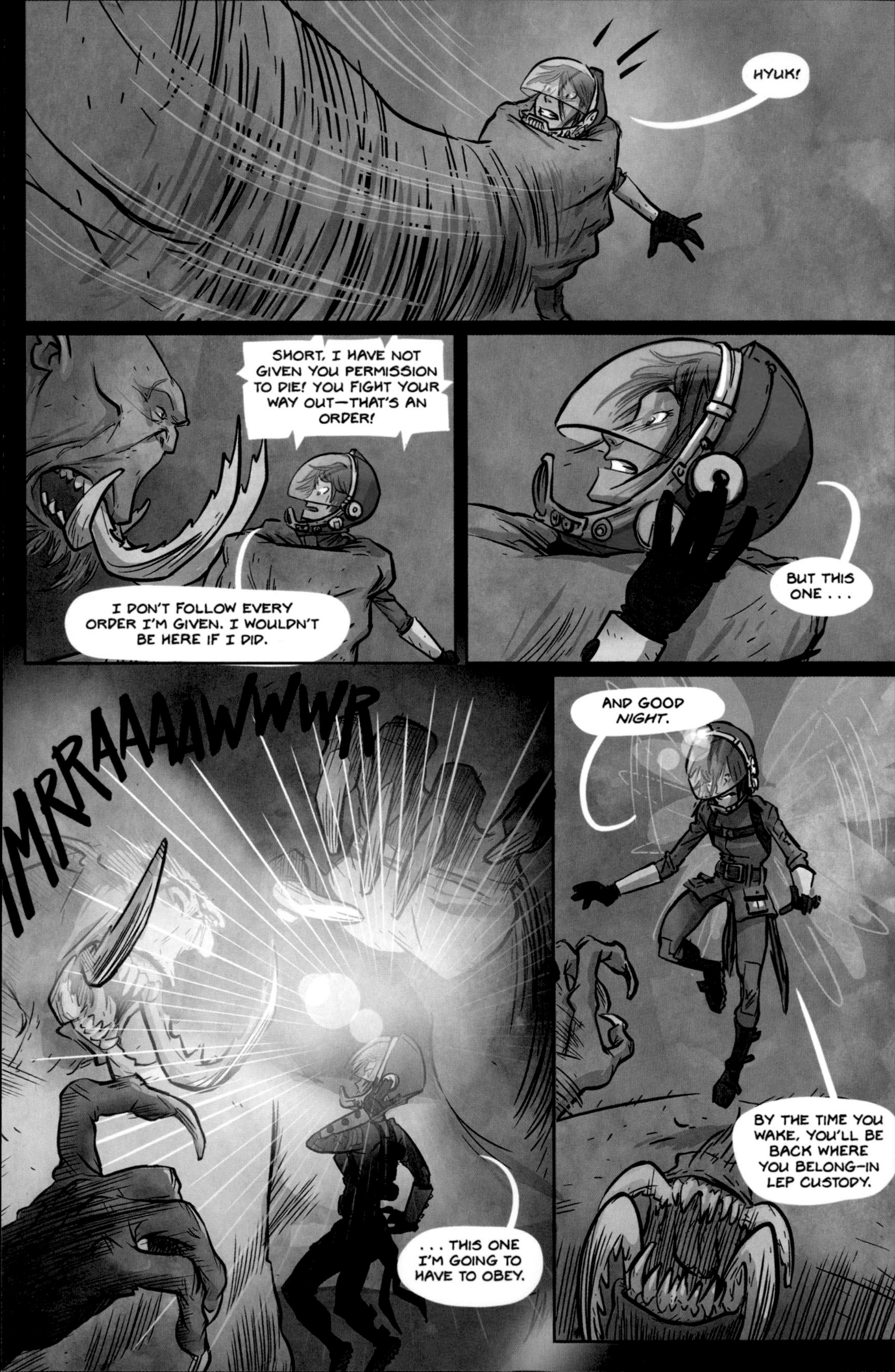
HYUK!
SHORT, I HAVE NOT GIVEN YOU PERMISSION TO DIE! YOU FIGHT YOUR WAY OUT—THAT'S AN ORDER!
I DON'T FOLLOW EVERY ORDER I'M GIVEN. I WOULDN'T BE HERE IF I DID.
BUT THIS ONE . . .
MRRAAAAWWWR
. . . THIS ONE I'M GOING TO HAVE TO OBEY.
AND GOOD NIGHT.
BY THE TIME YOU WAKE, YOU'LL BE BACK WHERE YOU BELONG—IN LEP CUSTODY.

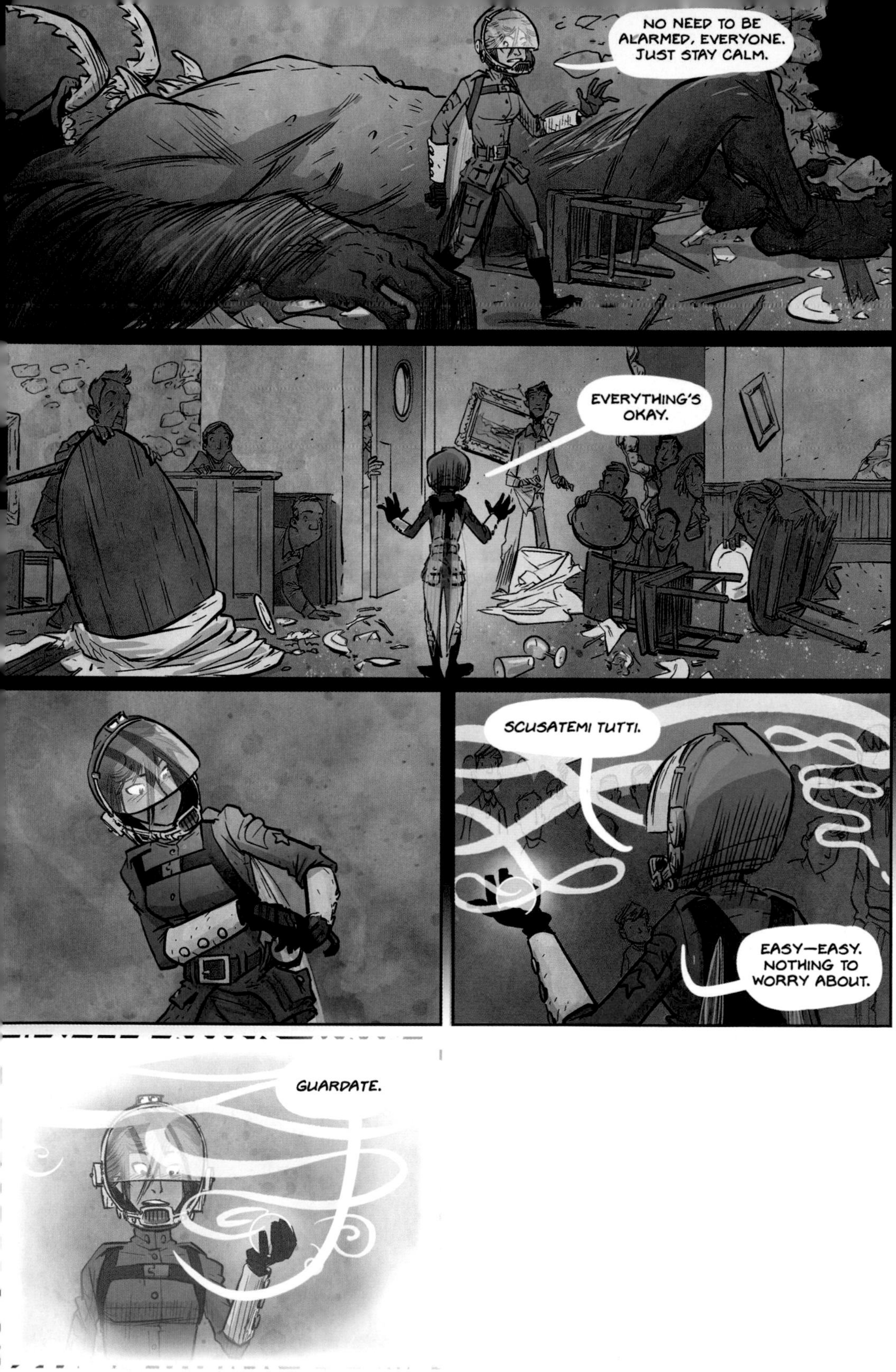
NO NEED TO BE ALARMED, EVERYONE. JUST STAY CALM.
EVERYTHING'S OKAY.
SCUSATEMI TUTTI.
EASY—EASY. NOTHING TO WORRY ABOUT.
GUARDATE.

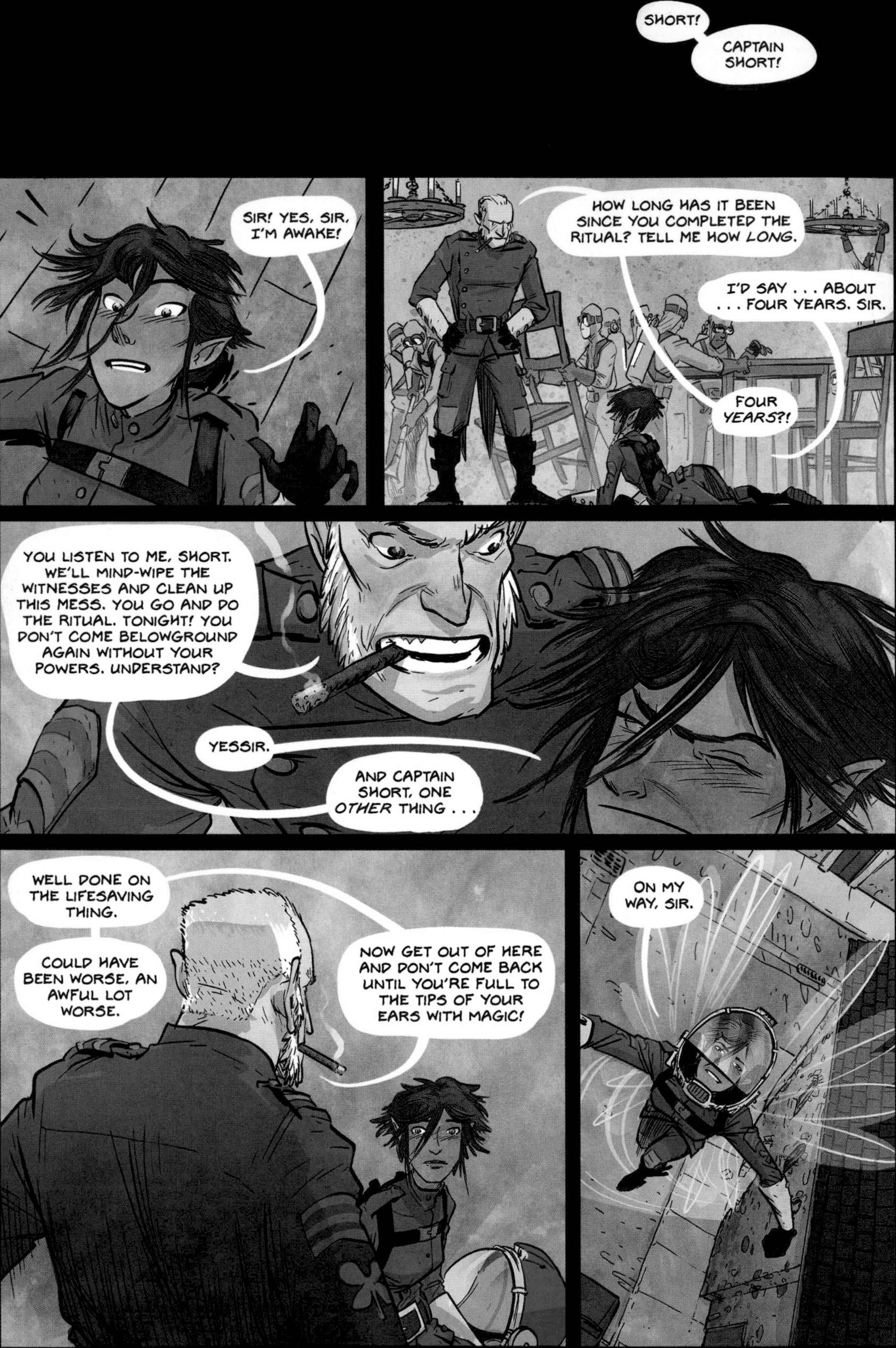
SHORT!
CAPTAIN SHORT!
SIR! YES, SIR, I'M AWAKE!
HOW LONG HAS IT BEEN SINCE YOU COMPLETED THE RITUAL? TELL ME HOW *LONG*.
I'D SAY . . . ABOUT . . . FOUR YEARS. SIR.
FOUR *YEARS*?!
YOU LISTEN TO ME, SHORT. WE'LL MIND-WIPE THE WITNESSES AND CLEAN UP THIS MESS. YOU GO AND DO THE RITUAL. TONIGHT! YOU DON'T COME BELOWGROUND AGAIN WITHOUT YOUR POWERS. UNDERSTAND?
YESSIR.
AND CAPTAIN SHORT, ONE *OTHER* THING . . .
WELL DONE ON THE LIFESAVING THING.
COULD HAVE BEEN WORSE, AN AWFUL LOT WORSE.
NOW GET OUT OF HERE AND DON'T COME BACK UNTIL YOU'RE FULL TO THE TIPS OF YOUR EARS WITH MAGIC!
ON MY WAY, SIR.

CHAPTER FOUR

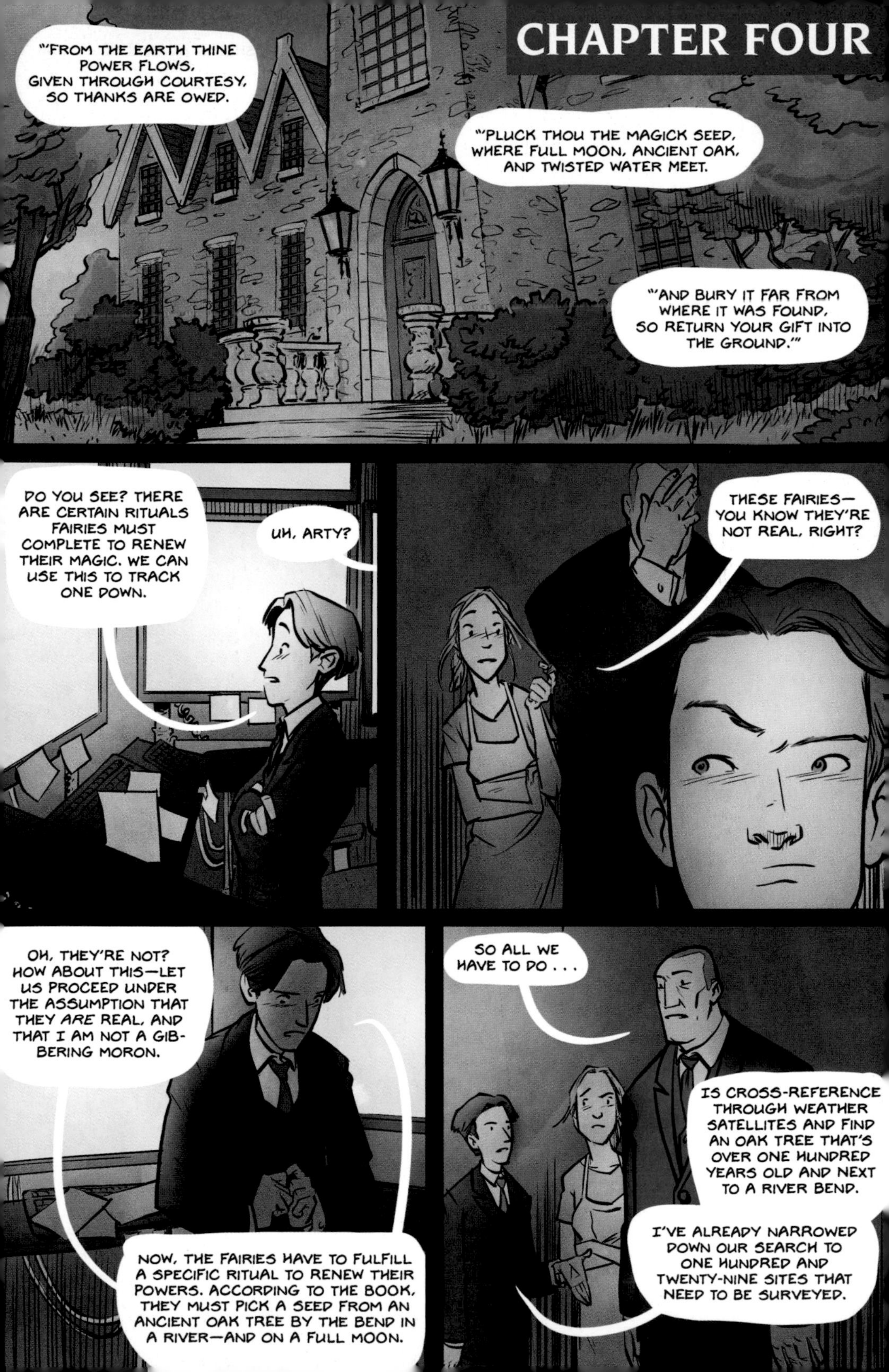
"'FROM THE EARTH THINE POWER FLOWS, GIVEN THROUGH COURTESY, SO THANKS ARE OWED.
"'PLUCK THOU THE MAGICK SEED, WHERE FULL MOON, ANCIENT OAK, AND TWISTED WATER MEET.
"'AND BURY IT FAR FROM WHERE IT WAS FOUND, SO RETURN YOUR GIFT INTO THE GROUND.'"
DO YOU SEE? THERE ARE CERTAIN RITUALS FAIRIES MUST COMPLETE TO RENEW THEIR MAGIC. WE CAN USE THIS TO TRACK ONE DOWN.
UH, ARTY?
THESE FAIRIES— YOU KNOW THEY'RE NOT REAL, RIGHT?
OH, THEY'RE NOT? HOW ABOUT THIS—LET US PROCEED UNDER THE ASSUMPTION THAT THEY *ARE* REAL, AND THAT I AM NOT A GIB-BERING MORON.
NOW, THE FAIRIES HAVE TO FULFILL A SPECIFIC RITUAL TO RENEW THEIR POWERS. ACCORDING TO THE BOOK, THEY MUST PICK A SEED FROM AN ANCIENT OAK TREE BY THE BEND IN A RIVER—AND ON A FULL MOON.
SO ALL WE HAVE TO DO . . .
IS CROSS-REFERENCE THROUGH WEATHER SATELLITES AND FIND AN OAK TREE THAT'S OVER ONE HUNDRED YEARS OLD AND NEXT TO A RIVER BEND.
I'VE ALREADY NARROWED DOWN OUR SEARCH TO ONE HUNDRED AND TWENTY-NINE SITES THAT NEED TO BE SURVEYED.

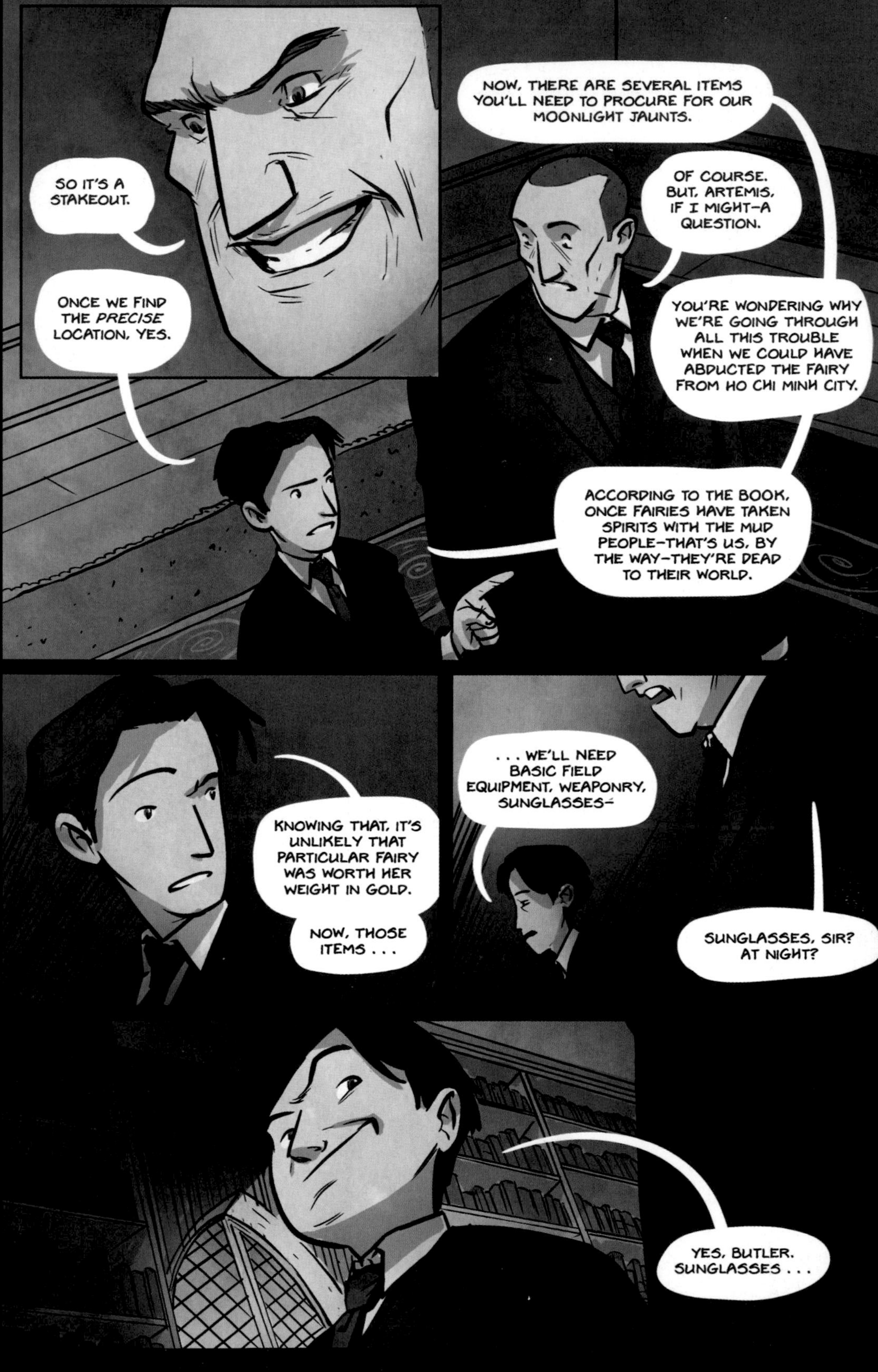
SO IT'S A STAKEOUT.
ONCE WE FIND THE *PRECISE* LOCATION, YES.
NOW, THERE ARE SEVERAL ITEMS YOU'LL NEED TO PROCURE FOR OUR MOONLIGHT JAUNTS.
OF COURSE. BUT, ARTEMIS, IF I MIGHT—A QUESTION.
YOU'RE WONDERING WHY WE'RE GOING THROUGH ALL THIS TROUBLE WHEN WE COULD HAVE ABDUCTED THE FAIRY FROM HO CHI MINH CITY.
ACCORDING TO THE BOOK, ONCE FAIRIES HAVE TAKEN SPIRITS WITH THE MUD PEOPLE—THAT'S US, BY THE WAY—THEY'RE DEAD TO THEIR WORLD.
KNOWING THAT, IT'S UNLIKELY THAT PARTICULAR FAIRY WAS WORTH HER WEIGHT IN GOLD.
NOW, THOSE ITEMS . . .
. . . WE'LL NEED BASIC FIELD EQUIPMENT, WEAPONRY, SUNGLASSES—
SUNGLASSES, SIR? AT NIGHT?
YES, BUTLER. SUNGLASSES . . .

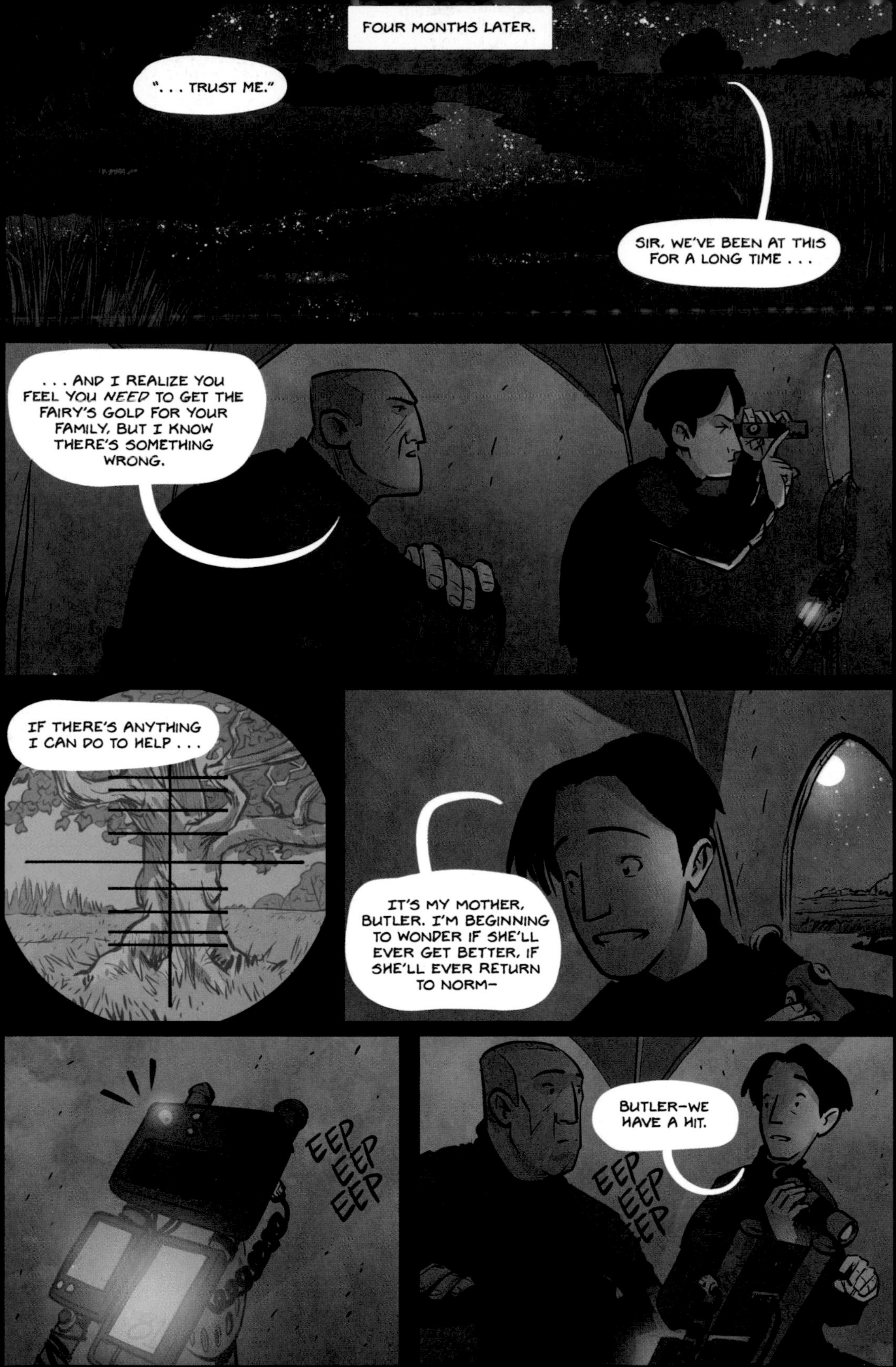
FOUR MONTHS LATER.
". . . TRUST ME."
SIR, WE'VE BEEN AT THIS FOR A LONG TIME . . .
. . . AND I REALIZE YOU FEEL YOU *NEED* TO GET THE FAIRY'S GOLD FOR YOUR FAMILY, BUT I KNOW THERE'S SOMETHING WRONG.
IF THERE'S ANYTHING I CAN DO TO HELP . . .
IT'S MY MOTHER, BUTLER. I'M BEGINNING TO WONDER IF SHE'LL EVER GET BETTER, IF SHE'LL EVER RETURN TO NORM–
EEP EEP EEP
BUTLER–WE HAVE A HIT.
EEP EEP EEP

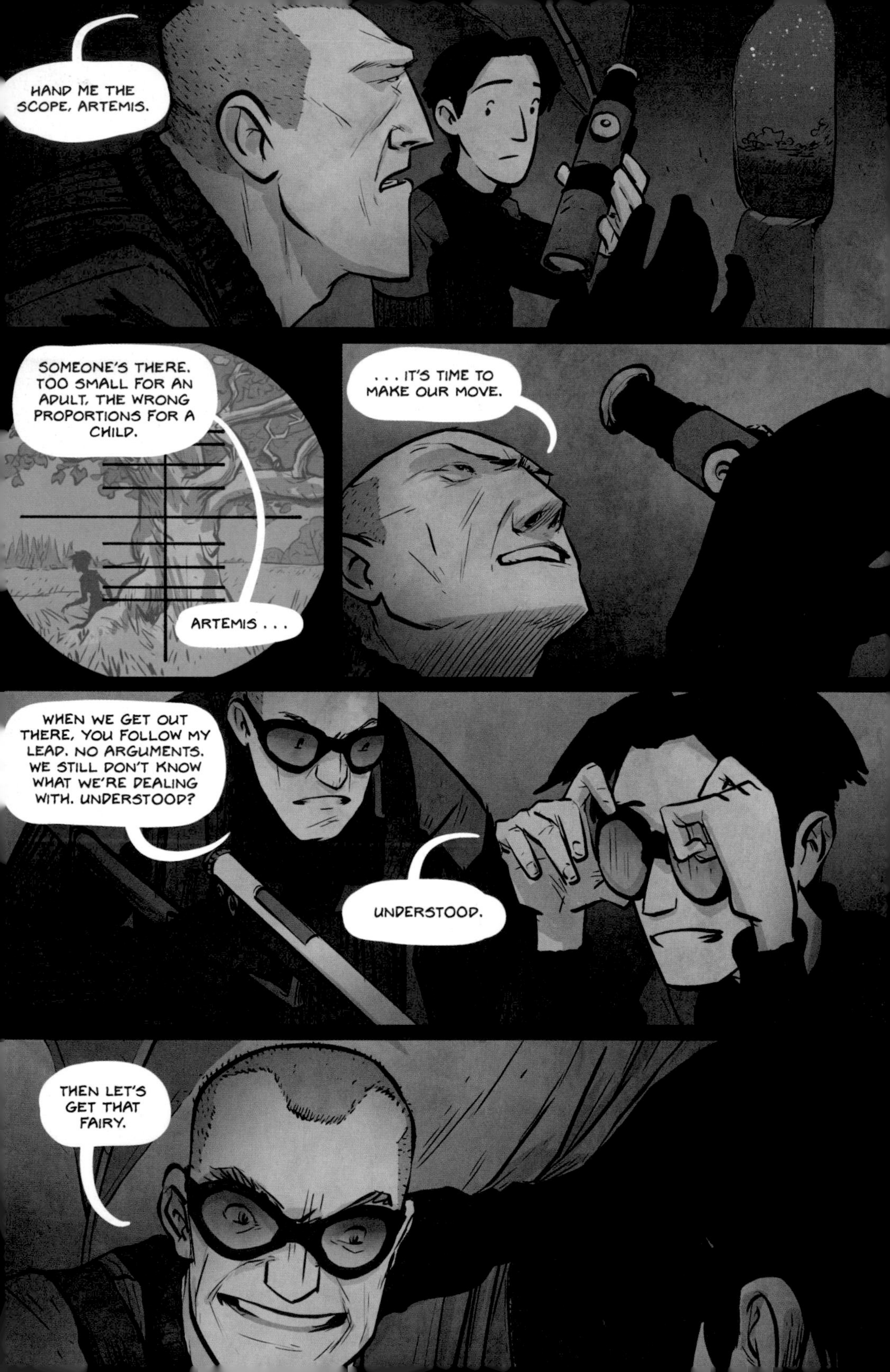
HAND ME THE SCOPE, ARTEMIS.
SOMEONE'S THERE. TOO SMALL FOR AN ADULT, THE WRONG PROPORTIONS FOR A CHILD.
ARTEMIS . . .
. . . IT'S TIME TO MAKE OUR MOVE.
WHEN WE GET OUT THERE, YOU FOLLOW MY LEAD. NO ARGUMENTS. WE STILL DON'T KNOW WHAT WE'RE DEALING WITH. UNDERSTOOD?
UNDERSTOOD.
THEN LET'S GET THAT FAIRY.

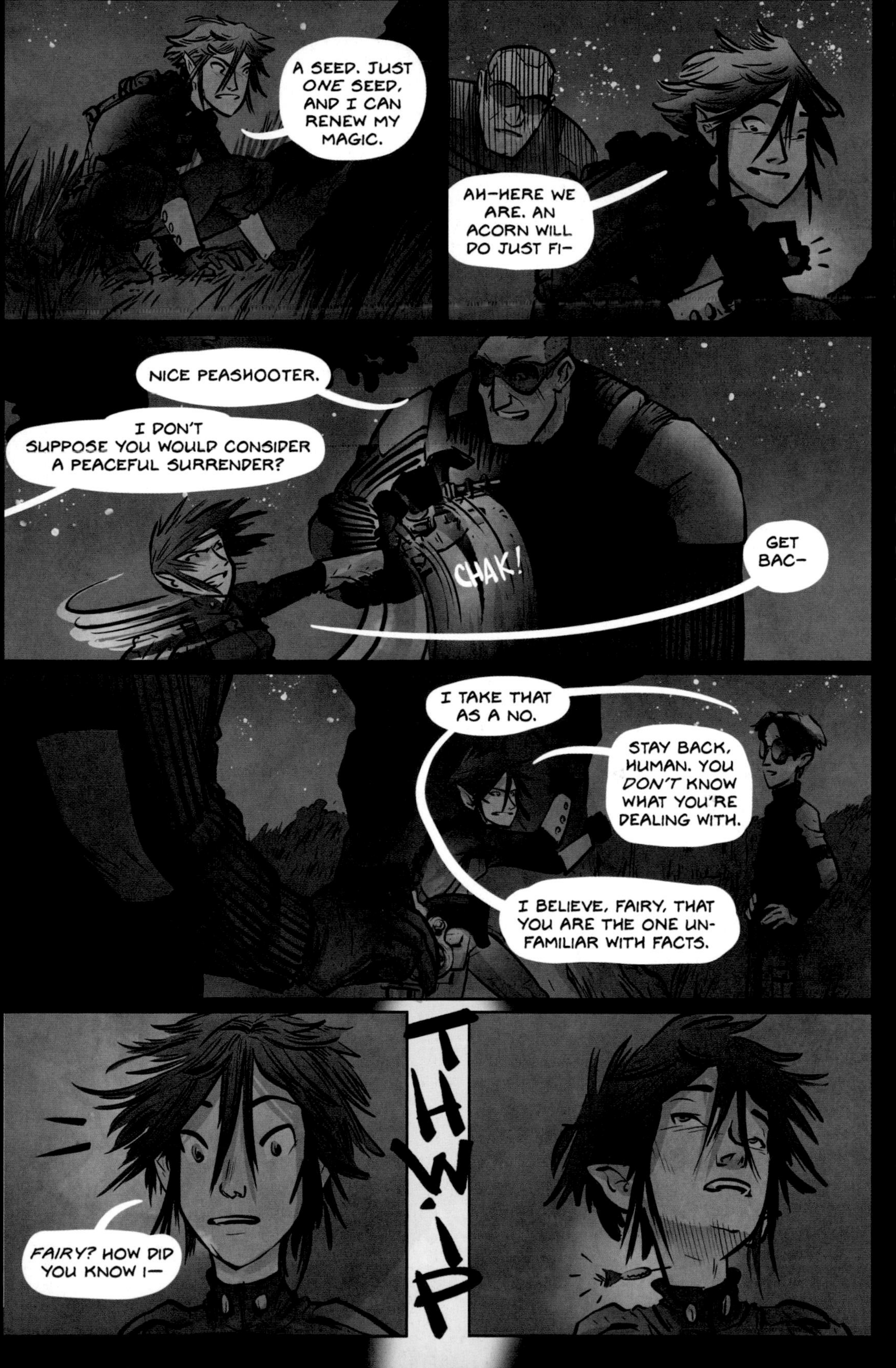
A SEED. JUST *ONE* SEED, AND I CAN RENEW MY MAGIC.
AH—HERE WE ARE. AN ACORN WILL DO JUST FI—
NICE PEASHOOTER.
I DON'T SUPPOSE YOU WOULD CONSIDER A PEACEFUL SURRENDER?
CHAK!
GET BAC—
I TAKE THAT AS A NO.
STAY BACK, HUMAN. YOU *DON'T* KNOW WHAT YOU'RE DEALING WITH.
I BELIEVE, FAIRY, THAT YOU ARE THE ONE UN-FAMILIAR WITH FACTS.
FAIRY? HOW DID YOU KNOW I—
THWIP

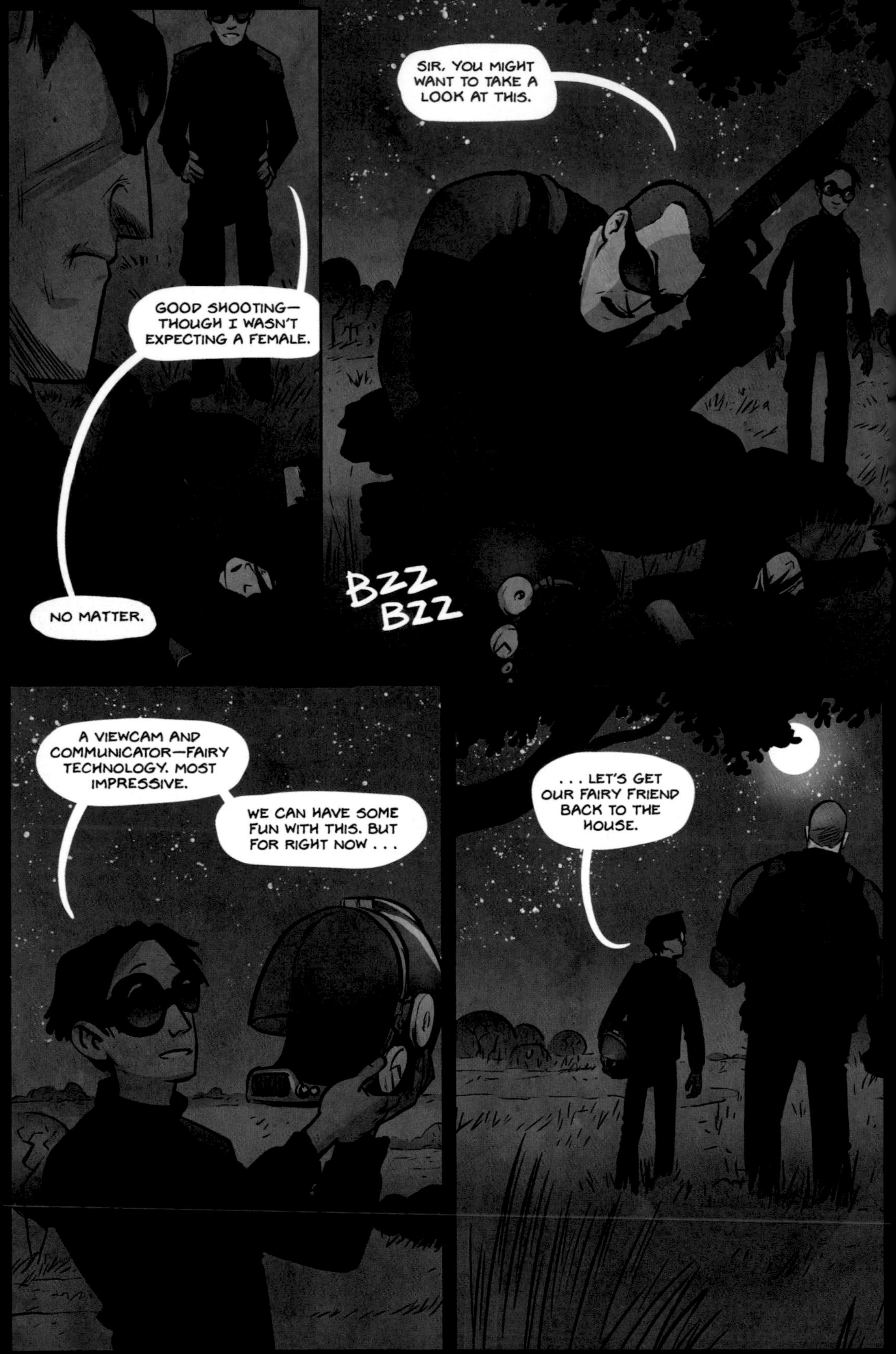
SIR, YOU MIGHT WANT TO TAKE A LOOK AT THIS.
GOOD SHOOTING—THOUGH I WASN'T EXPECTING A FEMALE.
NO MATTER.
BZZ BZZ
A VIEWCAM AND COMMUNICATOR—FAIRY TECHNOLOGY. MOST IMPRESSIVE.
WE CAN HAVE SOME FUN WITH THIS. BUT FOR RIGHT NOW . . .
. . . LET'S GET OUR FAIRY FRIEND BACK TO THE HOUSE.

CHAPTER FIVE

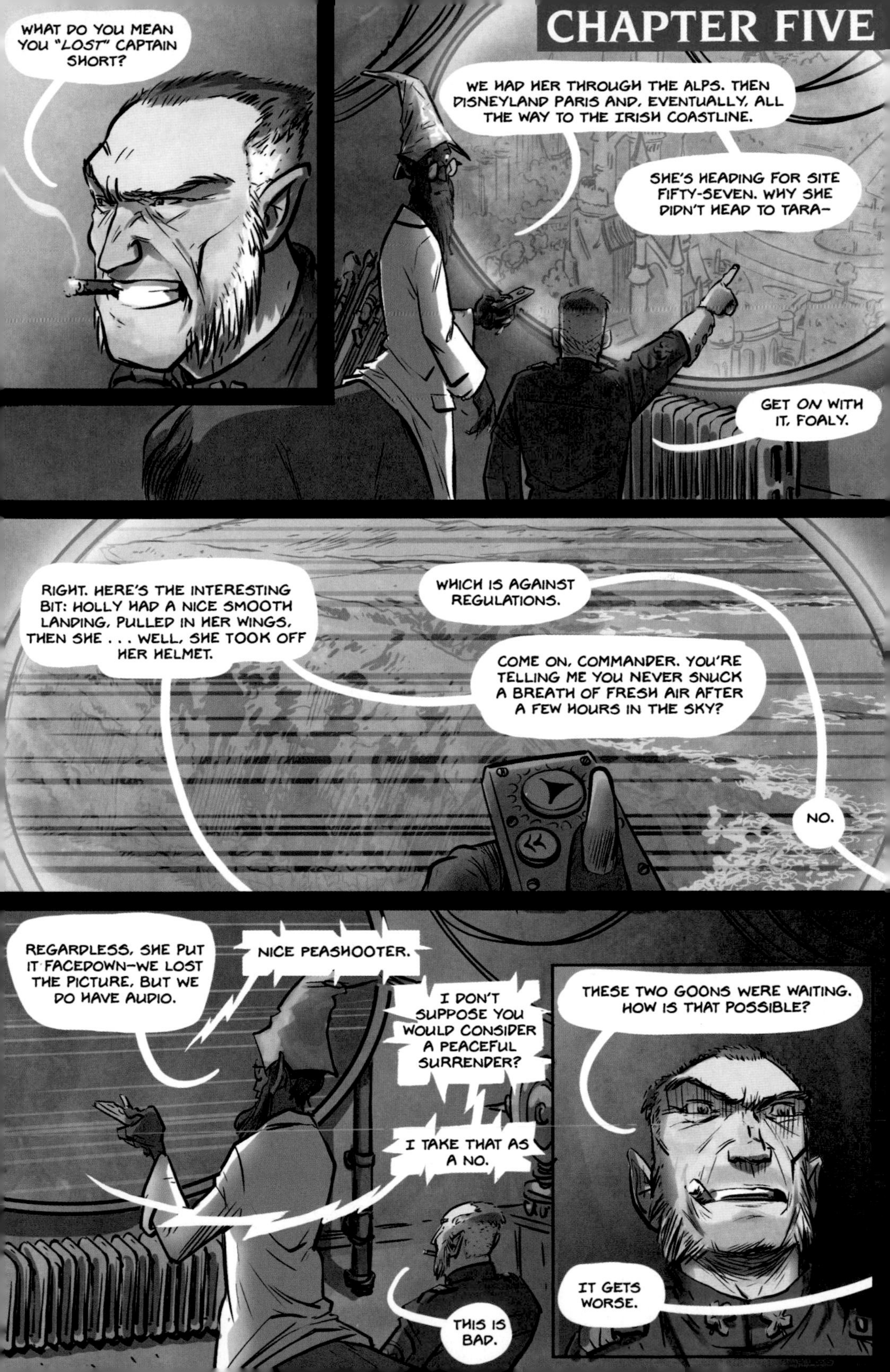

WHAT DO YOU MEAN YOU "LOST" CAPTAIN SHORT?
WE HAD HER THROUGH THE ALPS. THEN DISNEYLAND PARIS AND, EVENTUALLY, ALL THE WAY TO THE IRISH COASTLINE.
SHE'S HEADING FOR SITE FIFTY-SEVEN. WHY SHE DIDN'T HEAD TO TARA—
GET ON WITH IT, FOALY.
RIGHT. HERE'S THE INTERESTING BIT: HOLLY HAD A NICE SMOOTH LANDING, PULLED IN HER WINGS, THEN SHE . . . WELL, SHE TOOK OFF HER HELMET.
WHICH IS AGAINST REGULATIONS.
COME ON, COMMANDER. YOU'RE TELLING ME YOU NEVER SNUCK A BREATH OF FRESH AIR AFTER A FEW HOURS IN THE SKY?
NO.
REGARDLESS, SHE PUT IT FACEDOWN—WE LOST THE PICTURE, BUT WE DO HAVE AUDIO.
NICE PEASHOOTER.
I DON'T SUPPOSE YOU WOULD CONSIDER A PEACEFUL SURRENDER?
I TAKE THAT AS A NO.
THIS IS BAD.
THESE TWO GOONS WERE WAITING. HOW IS THAT POSSIBLE?
IT GETS WORSE.

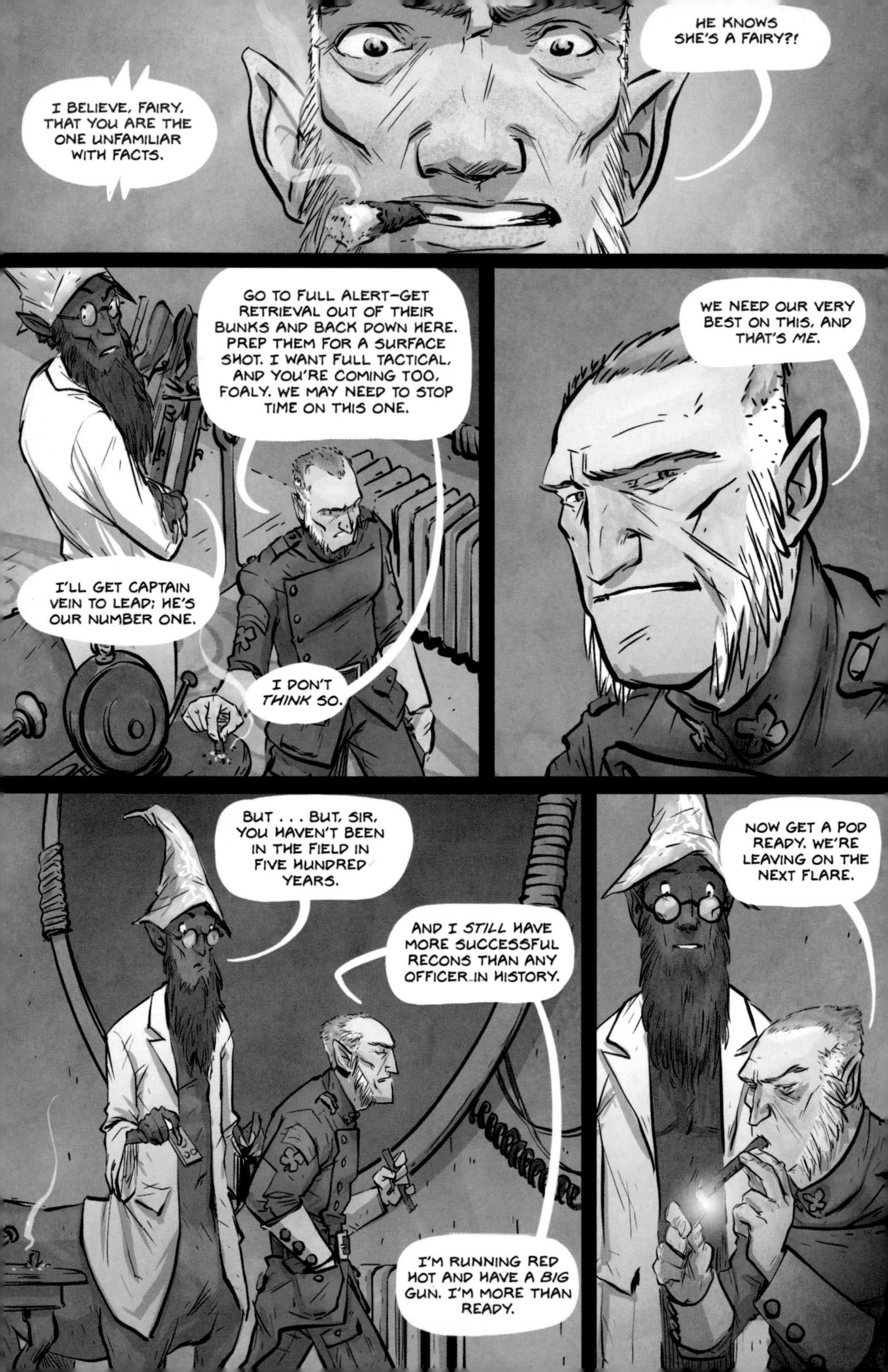
I BELIEVE, FAIRY, THAT YOU ARE THE ONE UNFAMILIAR WITH FACTS.
HE KNOWS SHE'S A FAIRY?!
GO TO FULL ALERT—GET RETRIEVAL OUT OF THEIR BUNKS AND BACK DOWN HERE. PREP THEM FOR A SURFACE SHOT. I WANT FULL TACTICAL, AND YOU'RE COMING TOO, FOALY. WE MAY NEED TO STOP TIME ON THIS ONE.
I'LL GET CAPTAIN VEIN TO LEAD; HE'S OUR NUMBER ONE.
I DON'T *THINK* SO.
WE NEED OUR VERY BEST ON THIS, AND THAT'S *ME*.
BUT . . . BUT, SIR, YOU HAVEN'T BEEN IN THE FIELD IN FIVE HUNDRED YEARS.
AND I *STILL* HAVE MORE SUCCESSFUL RECONS THAN ANY OFFICER IN HISTORY.
I'M RUNNING RED HOT AND HAVE A *BIG* GUN. I'M MORE THAN READY.
NOW GET A POD READY. WE'RE LEAVING ON THE NEXT FLARE.

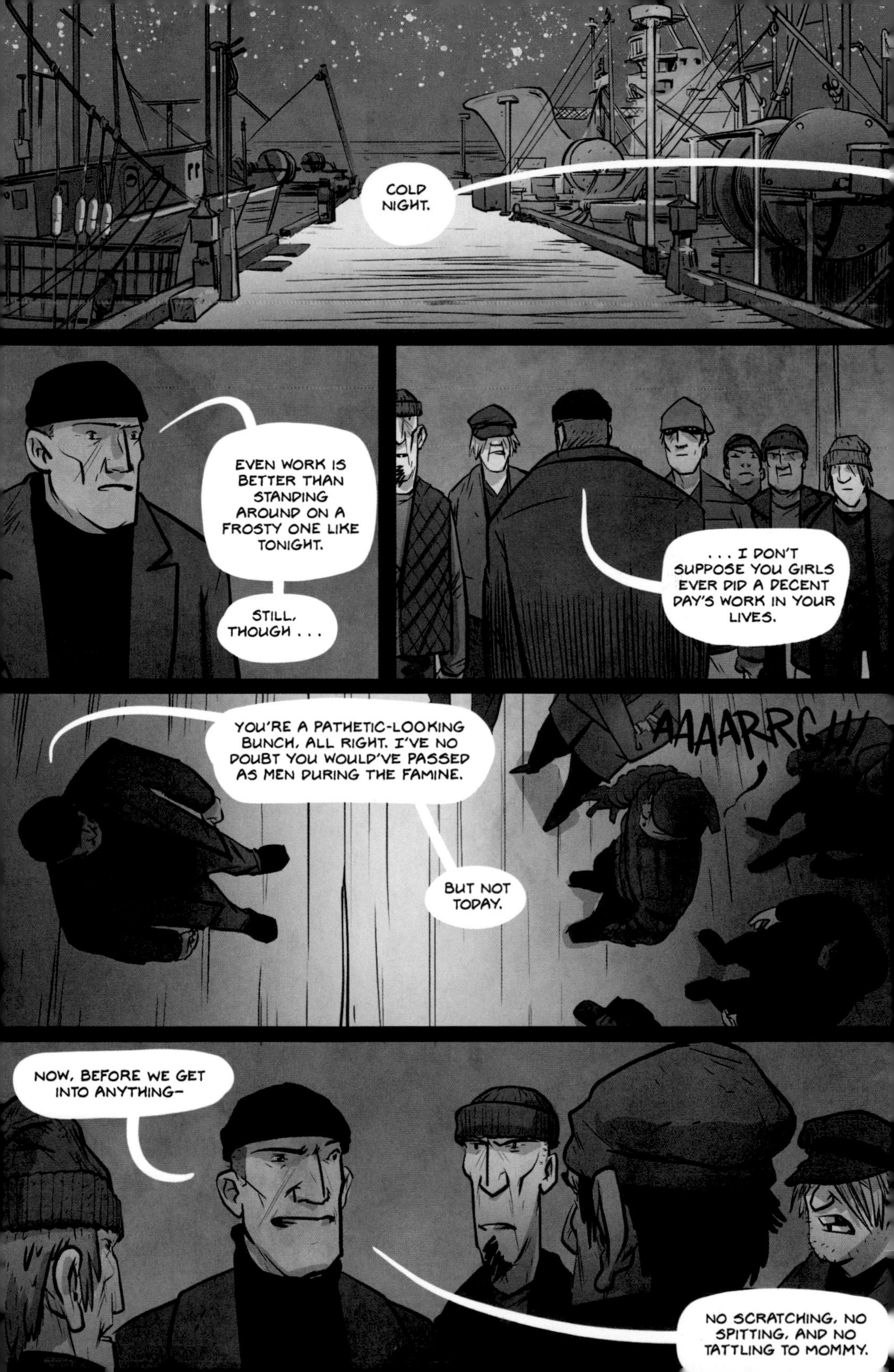
COLD NIGHT.
EVEN WORK IS BETTER THAN STANDING AROUND ON A FROSTY ONE LIKE TONIGHT.
STILL, THOUGH . . .
. . . I DON'T SUPPOSE YOU GIRLS EVER DID A DECENT DAY'S WORK IN YOUR LIVES.
YOU'RE A PATHETIC-LOOKING BUNCH, ALL RIGHT. I'VE NO DOUBT YOU WOULD'VE PASSED AS MEN DURING THE FAMINE.
AAAARRGH!!
BUT NOT TODAY.
NOW, BEFORE WE GET INTO ANYTHING—
NO SCRATCHING, NO SPITTING, AND NO TATTLING TO MOMMY.

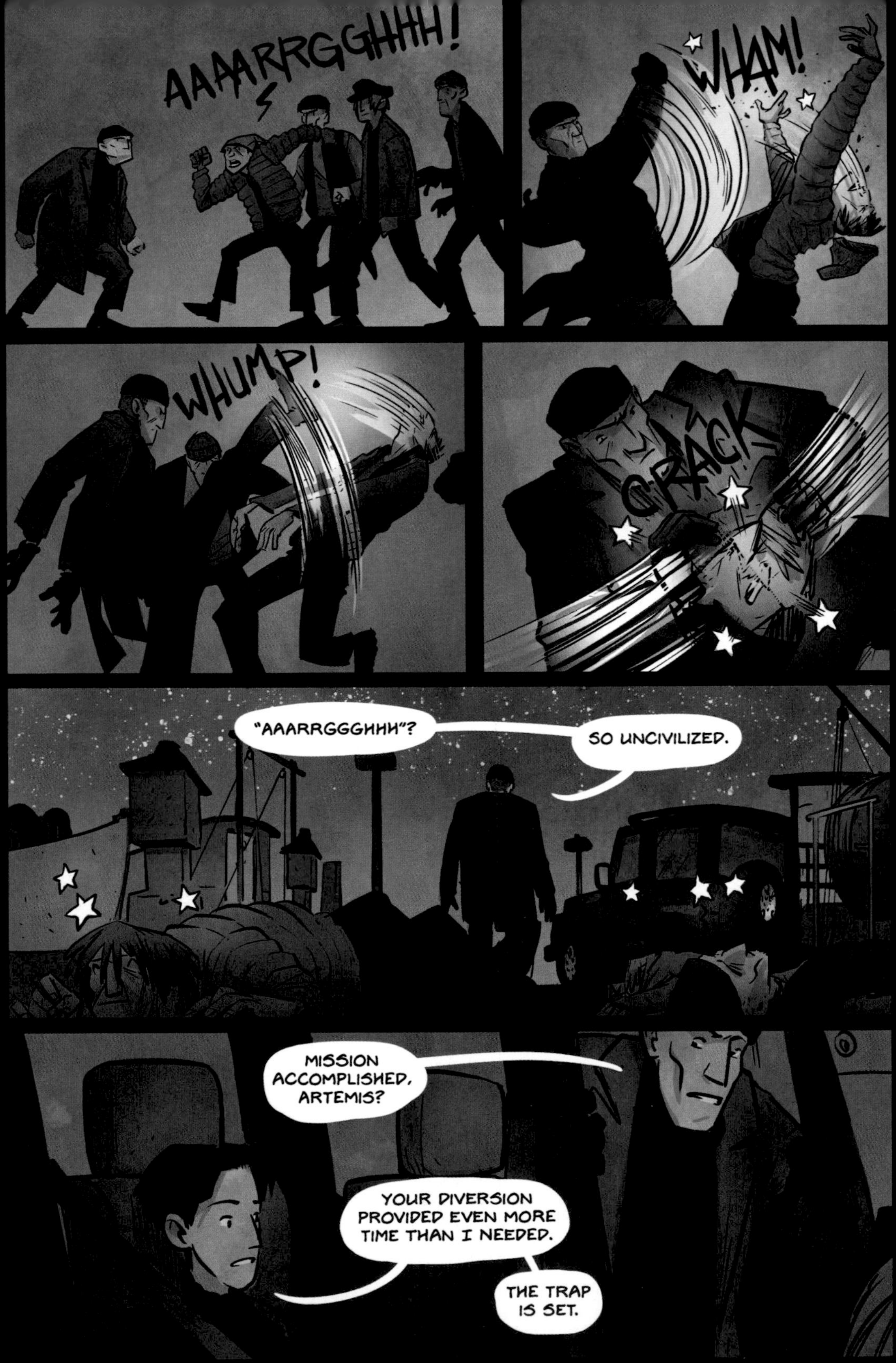
AAAARRGGHHH!
WHAM!
WHUMP!
CRACK
"AAARRGGGHHH"?
SO UNCIVILIZED.
MISSION ACCOMPLISHED, ARTEMIS?
YOUR DIVERSION PROVIDED EVEN MORE TIME THAN I NEEDED.
THE TRAP IS SET.

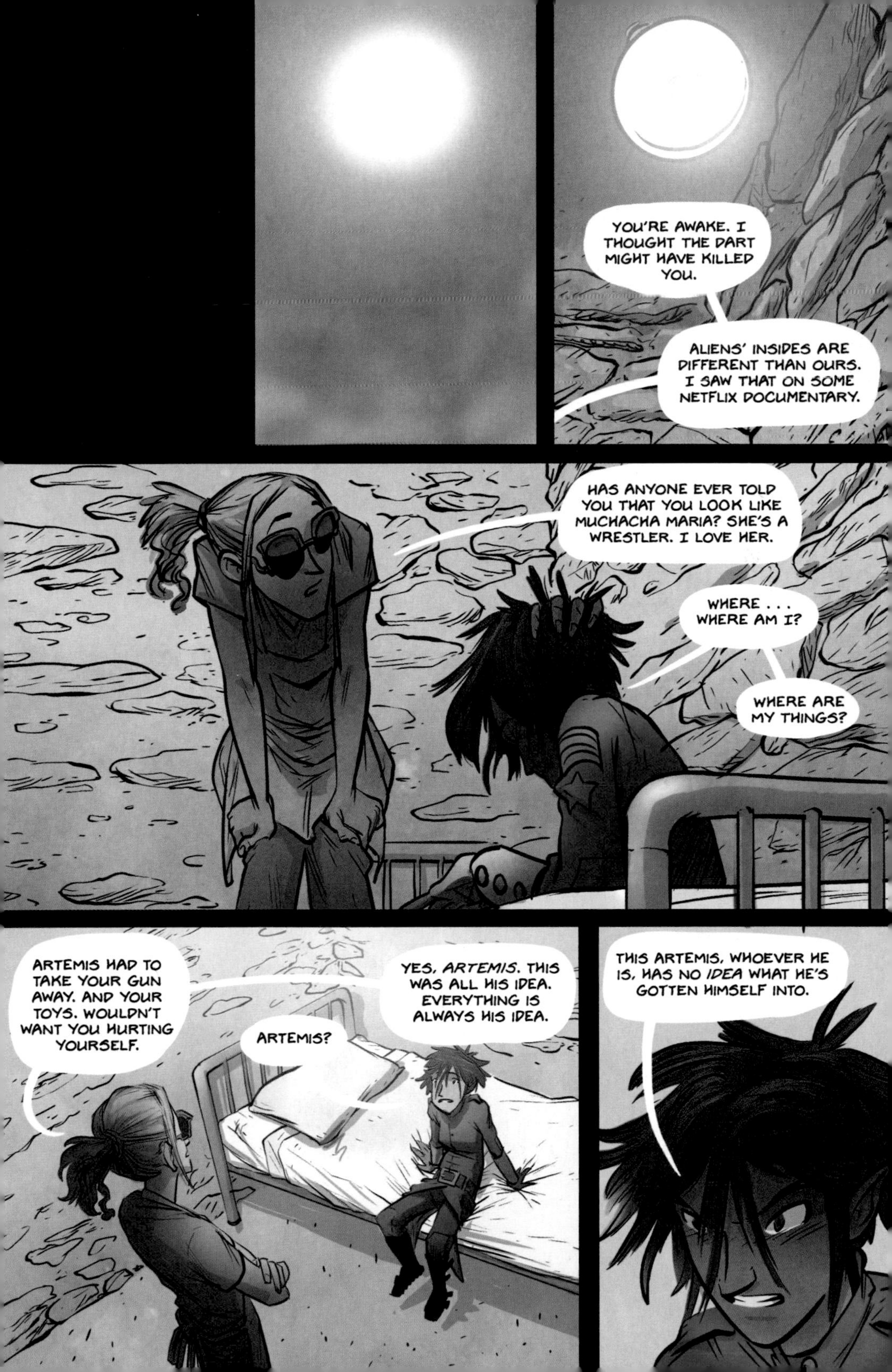
YOU'RE AWAKE. I THOUGHT THE DART MIGHT HAVE KILLED YOU.
ALIENS' INSIDES ARE DIFFERENT THAN OURS. I SAW THAT ON SOME NETFLIX DOCUMENTARY.
HAS ANYONE EVER TOLD YOU THAT YOU LOOK LIKE MUCHACHA MARIA? SHE'S A WRESTLER. I LOVE HER.
WHERE . . . WHERE AM I?
WHERE ARE MY THINGS?
ARTEMIS HAD TO TAKE YOUR GUN AWAY. AND YOUR TOYS. WOULDN'T WANT YOU HURTING YOURSELF.
ARTEMIS?
YES, *ARTEMIS*. THIS WAS ALL HIS IDEA. EVERYTHING IS ALWAYS HIS IDEA.
THIS ARTEMIS, WHOEVER HE IS, HAS NO *IDEA* WHAT HE'S GOTTEN HIMSELF INTO.

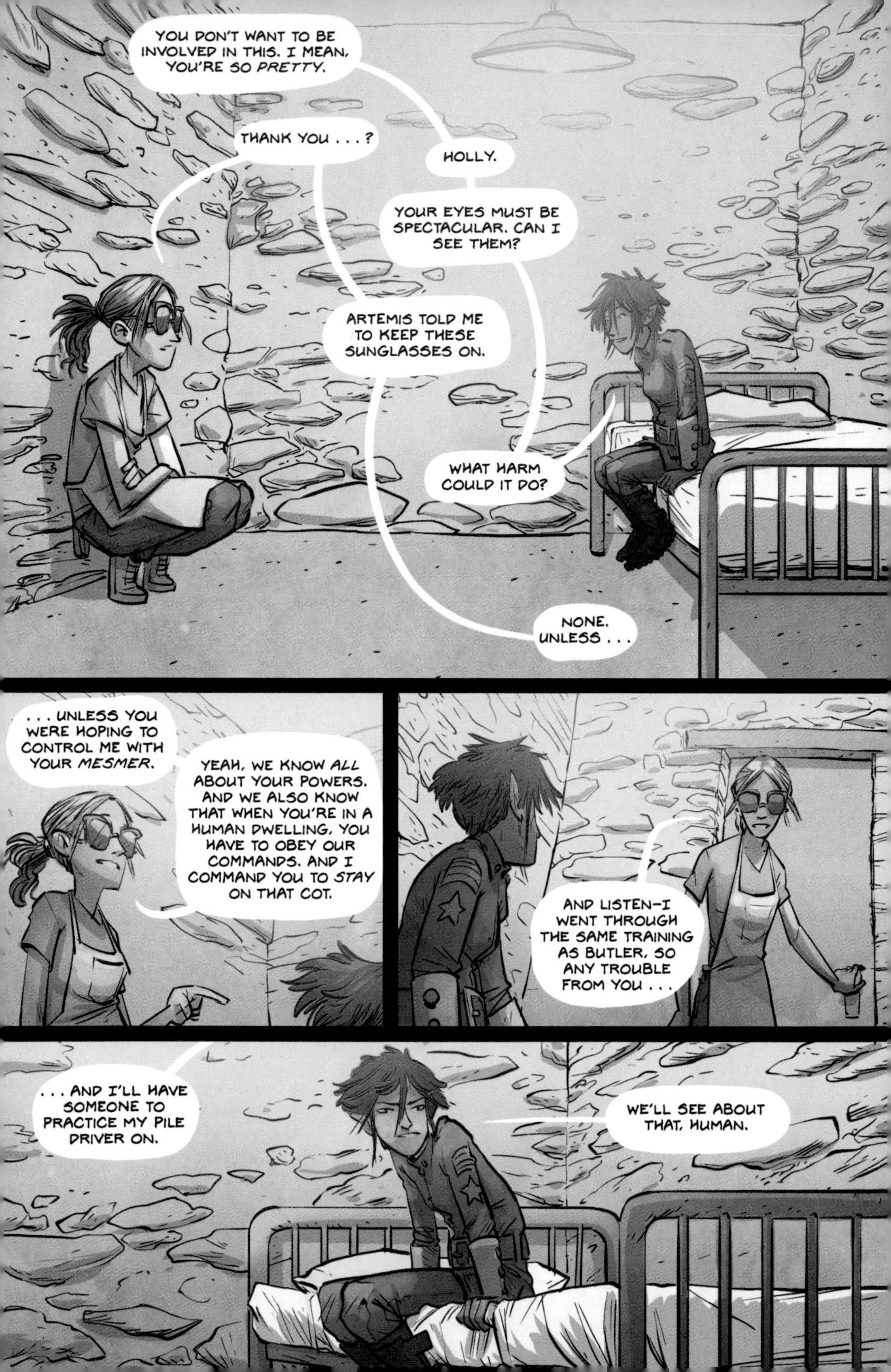
YOU DON'T WANT TO BE INVOLVED IN THIS. I MEAN, YOU'RE SO *PRETTY*.
THANK YOU . . . ?
HOLLY.
YOUR EYES MUST BE SPECTACULAR. CAN I SEE THEM?
ARTEMIS TOLD ME TO KEEP THESE SUNGLASSES ON.
WHAT HARM COULD IT DO?
NONE. UNLESS . . .
. . . UNLESS YOU WERE HOPING TO CONTROL ME WITH YOUR *MESMER*.
YEAH, WE KNOW *ALL* ABOUT YOUR POWERS. AND WE ALSO KNOW THAT WHEN YOU'RE IN A HUMAN DWELLING, YOU HAVE TO OBEY OUR COMMANDS. AND I COMMAND YOU TO *STAY* ON THAT COT.
AND LISTEN—I WENT THROUGH THE SAME TRAINING AS BUTLER, SO ANY TROUBLE FROM YOU . . .
. . . AND I'LL HAVE SOMEONE TO PRACTICE MY PILE DRIVER ON.
WE'LL SEE ABOUT THAT, HUMAN.

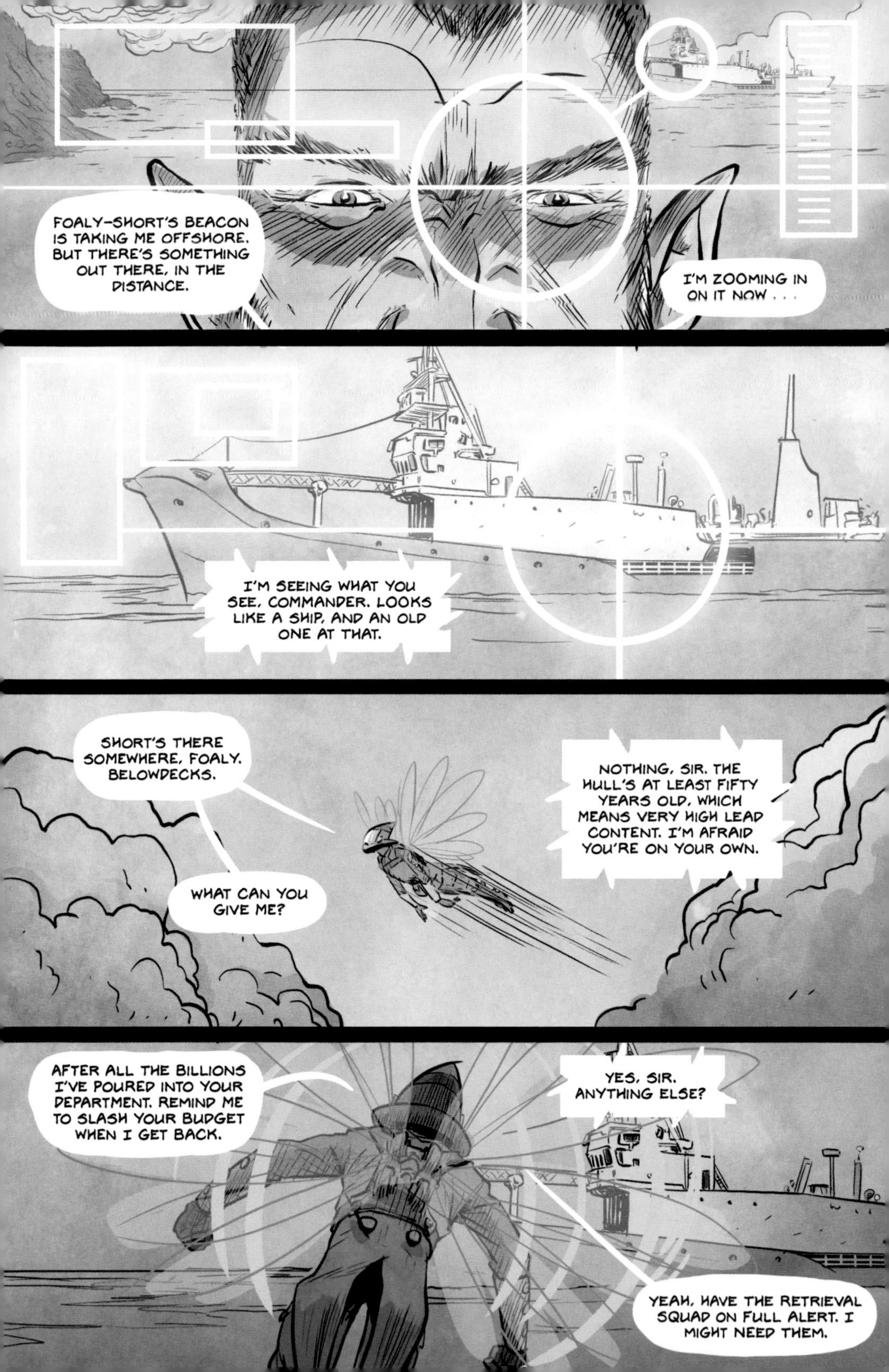
FOALY—SHORT'S BEACON IS TAKING ME OFFSHORE. BUT THERE'S SOMETHING OUT THERE, IN THE DISTANCE.
I'M ZOOMING IN ON IT NOW . . .
I'M SEEING WHAT YOU SEE, COMMANDER. LOOKS LIKE A SHIP, AND AN OLD ONE AT THAT.
SHORT'S THERE SOMEWHERE, FOALY. BELOWDECKS.
WHAT CAN YOU GIVE ME?
NOTHING, SIR. THE HULL'S AT LEAST FIFTY YEARS OLD, WHICH MEANS VERY HIGH LEAD CONTENT. I'M AFRAID YOU'RE ON YOUR OWN.
AFTER ALL THE BILLIONS I'VE POURED INTO YOUR DEPARTMENT. REMIND ME TO SLASH YOUR BUDGET WHEN I GET BACK.
YES, SIR. ANYTHING ELSE?
YEAH, HAVE THE RETRIEVAL SQUAD ON FULL ALERT. I MIGHT NEED THEM.

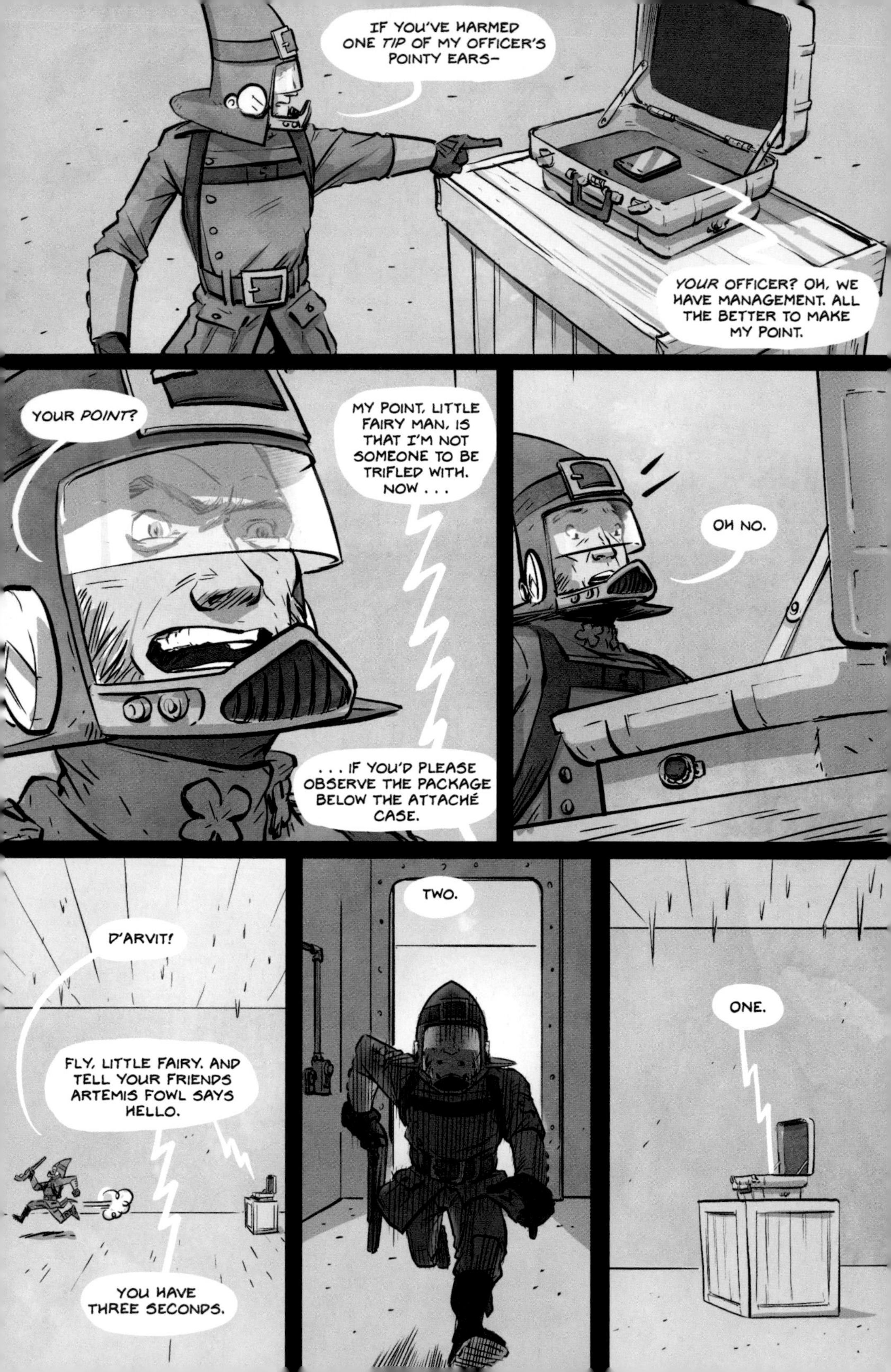
IF YOU'VE HARMED ONE *TIP* OF MY OFFICER'S POINTY EARS–
YOUR OFFICER? OH, WE HAVE MANAGEMENT. ALL THE BETTER TO MAKE MY POINT.
YOUR *POINT*?
MY POINT, LITTLE FAIRY MAN, IS THAT I'M NOT SOMEONE TO BE TRIFLED WITH. NOW . . .
. . . IF YOU'D PLEASE OBSERVE THE PACKAGE BELOW THE ATTACHÉ CASE.
OH NO.
D'ARVIT!
FLY, LITTLE FAIRY. AND TELL YOUR FRIENDS ARTEMIS FOWL SAYS HELLO.
YOU HAVE THREE SECONDS.
TWO.
ONE.

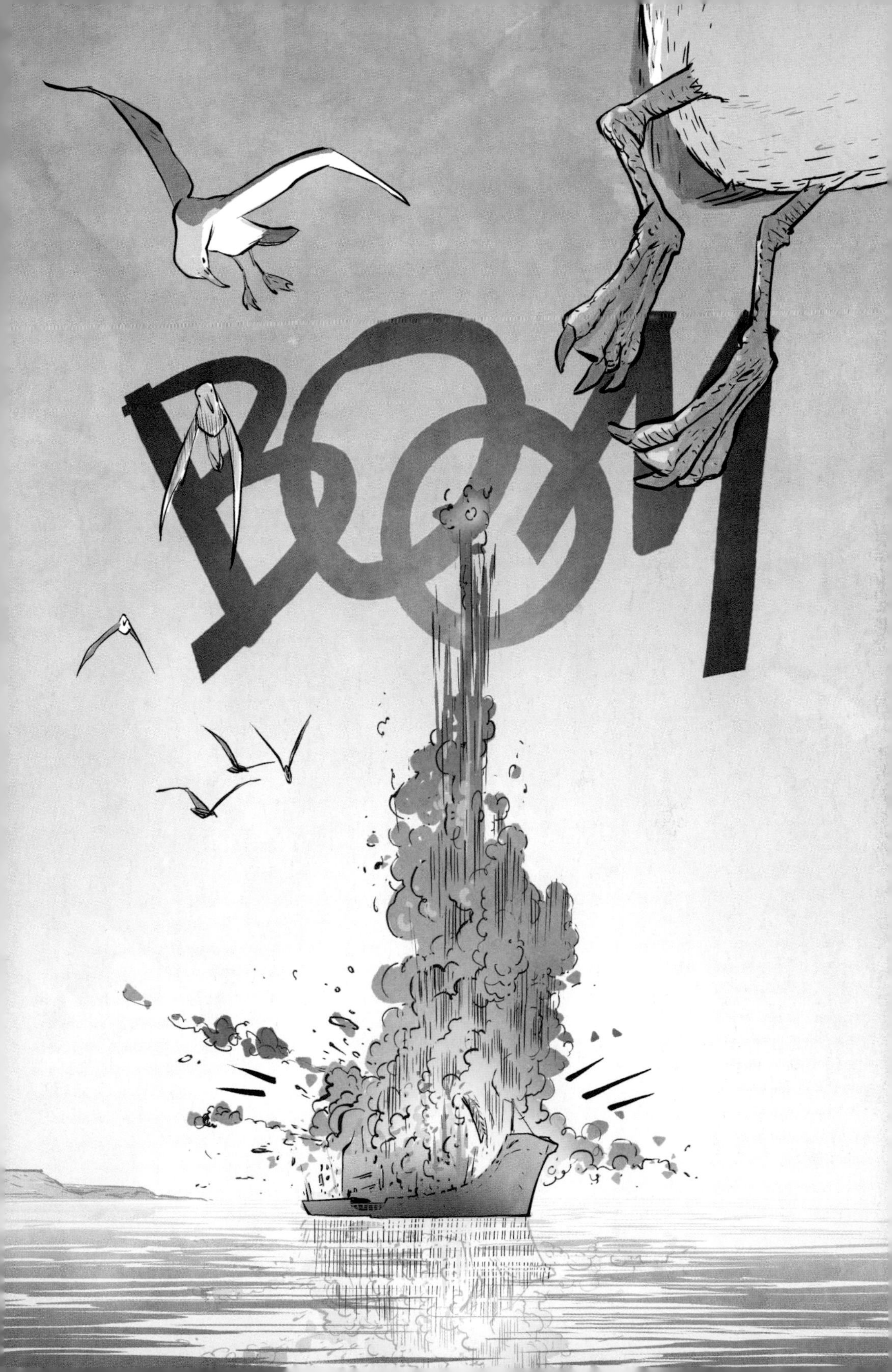
BOOM

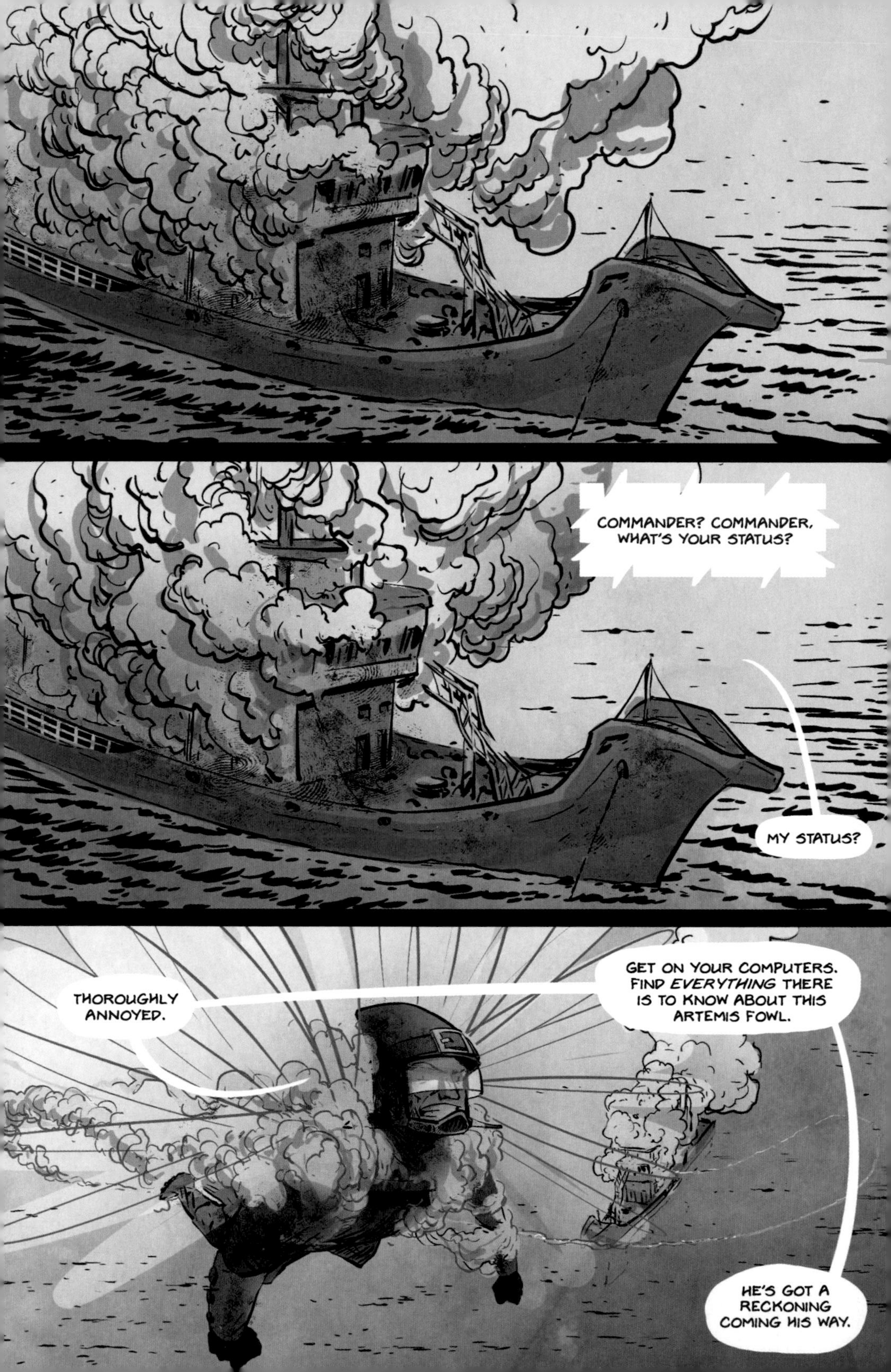
COMMANDER? COMMANDER, WHAT'S YOUR STATUS?
MY STATUS?
THOROUGHLY ANNOYED.
GET ON YOUR COMPUTERS. FIND *EVERYTHING* THERE IS TO KNOW ABOUT THIS ARTEMIS FOWL.
HE'S GOT A RECKONING COMING HIS WAY.

CHAPTER SIX

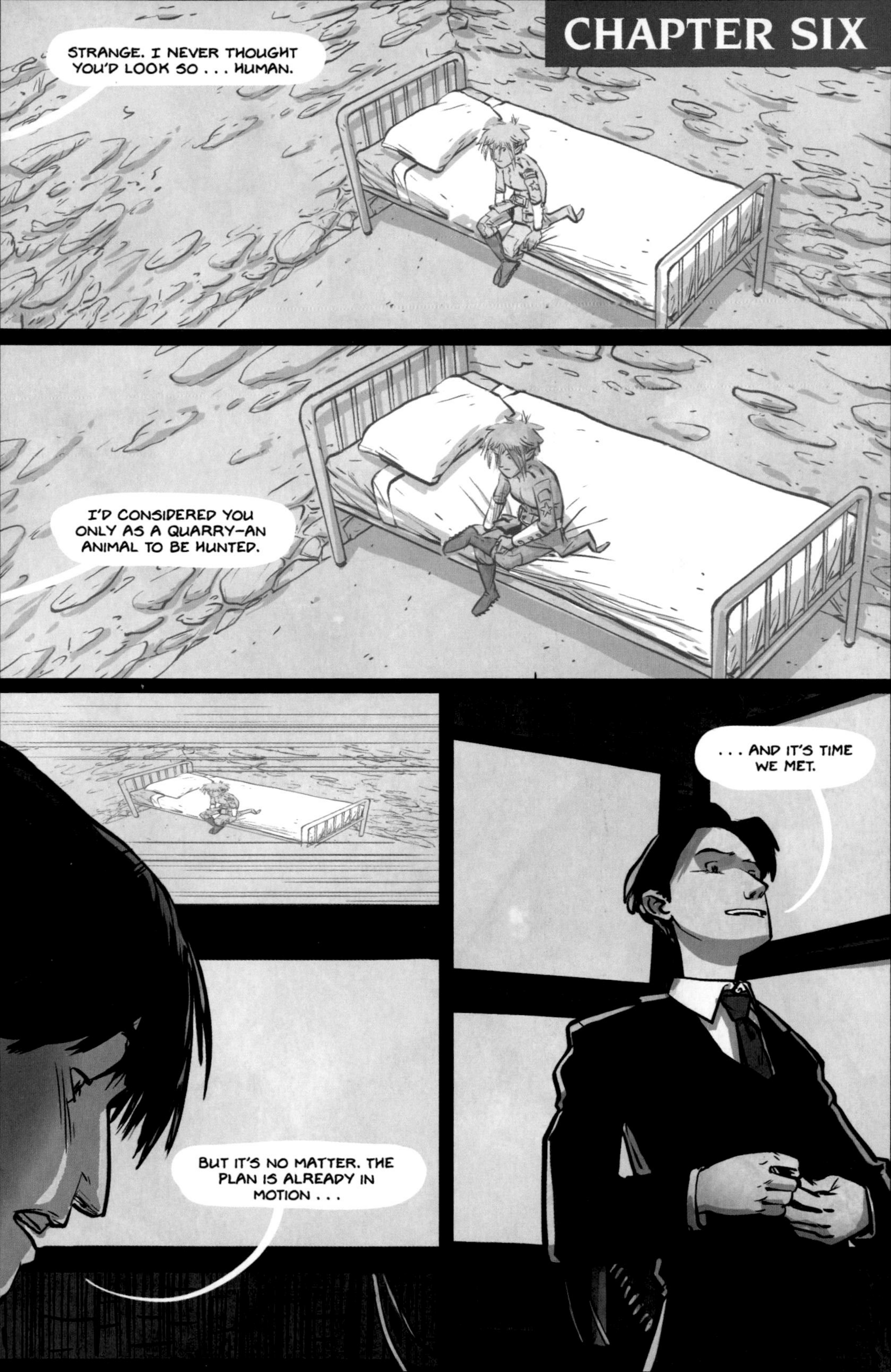
STRANGE. I NEVER THOUGHT YOU'D LOOK SO . . . HUMAN.
I'D CONSIDERED YOU ONLY AS A QUARRY—AN ANIMAL TO BE HUNTED.
BUT IT'S NO MATTER. THE PLAN IS ALREADY IN MOTION . . .
. . . AND IT'S TIME WE MET.

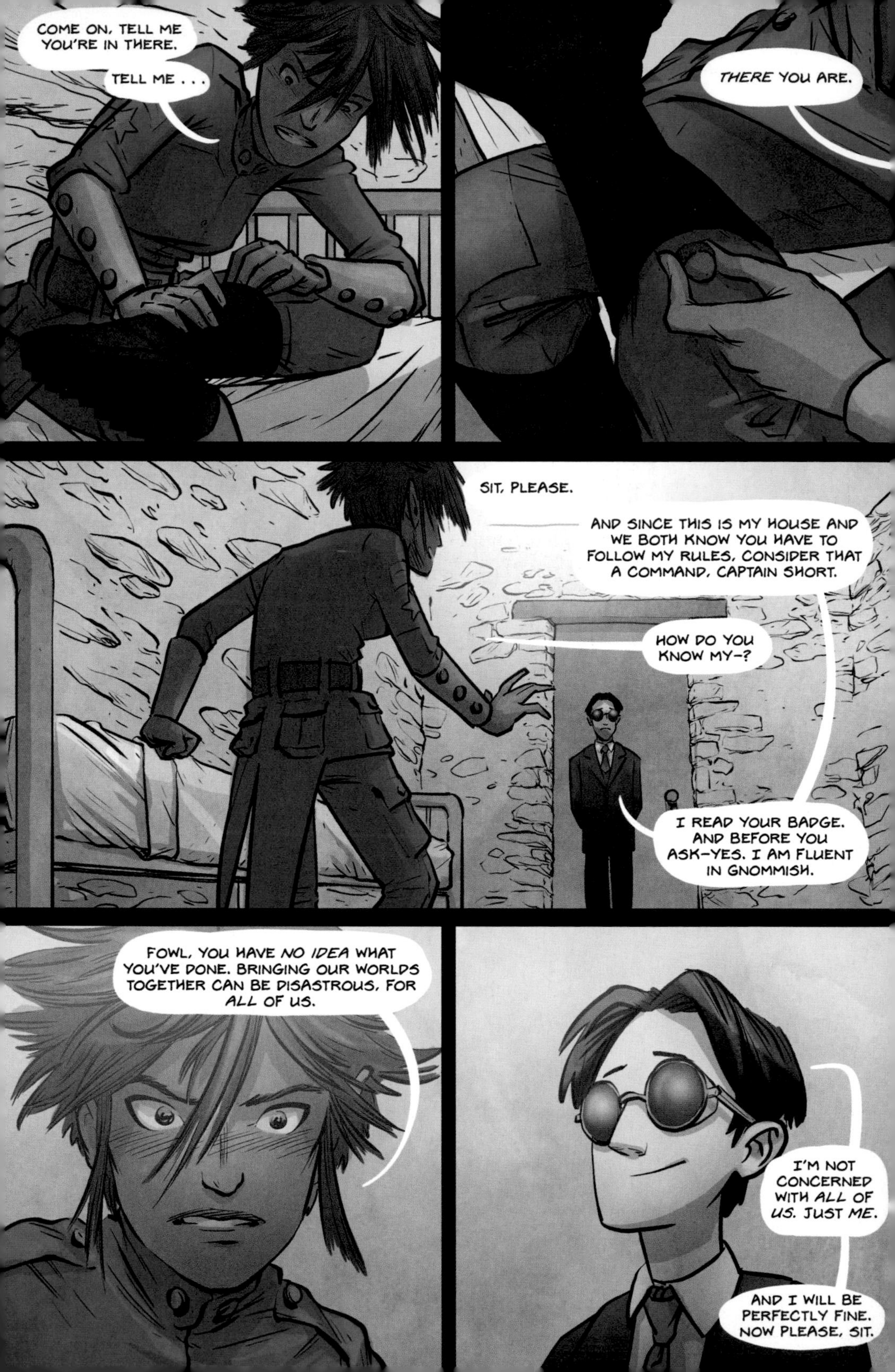
COME ON, TELL ME YOU'RE IN THERE.
TELL ME . . .
THERE YOU ARE.
SIT, PLEASE.
AND SINCE THIS IS MY HOUSE AND WE BOTH KNOW YOU HAVE TO FOLLOW MY RULES, CONSIDER THAT A COMMAND, CAPTAIN SHORT.
HOW DO YOU KNOW MY–?
I READ YOUR BADGE. AND BEFORE YOU ASK–YES. I AM FLUENT IN GNOMMISH.
FOWL, YOU HAVE *NO IDEA* WHAT YOU'VE DONE. BRINGING OUR WORLDS TOGETHER CAN BE DISASTROUS, FOR *ALL* OF US.
I'M NOT CONCERNED WITH *ALL OF US*. JUST *ME*.
AND I WILL BE PERFECTLY FINE. NOW PLEASE, SIT.

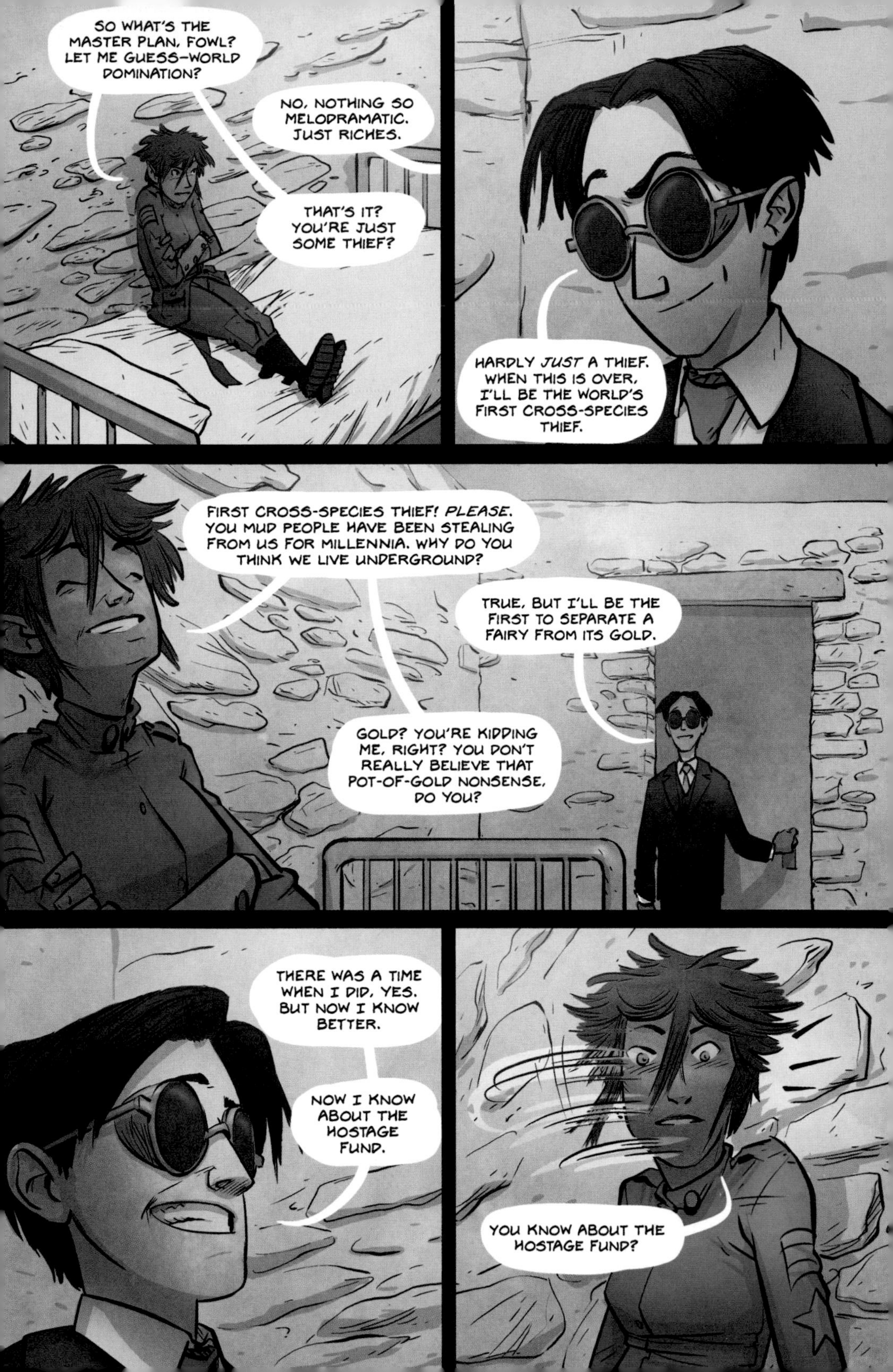
SO WHAT'S THE MASTER PLAN, FOWL? LET ME GUESS—WORLD DOMINATION?
NO, NOTHING SO MELODRAMATIC. JUST RICHES.
THAT'S IT? YOU'RE JUST SOME THIEF?
HARDLY *JUST* A THIEF. WHEN THIS IS OVER, I'LL BE THE WORLD'S FIRST CROSS-SPECIES THIEF.
FIRST CROSS-SPECIES THIEF! *PLEASE.* YOU MUD PEOPLE HAVE BEEN STEALING FROM US FOR MILLENNIA. WHY DO YOU THINK WE LIVE UNDERGROUND?
TRUE, BUT I'LL BE THE FIRST TO SEPARATE A FAIRY FROM ITS GOLD.
GOLD? YOU'RE KIDDING ME, RIGHT? YOU DON'T REALLY BELIEVE THAT POT-OF-GOLD NONSENSE, DO YOU?
THERE WAS A TIME WHEN I DID, YES. BUT NOW I KNOW BETTER.
NOW I KNOW ABOUT THE HOSTAGE FUND.
YOU KNOW ABOUT THE HOSTAGE FUND?

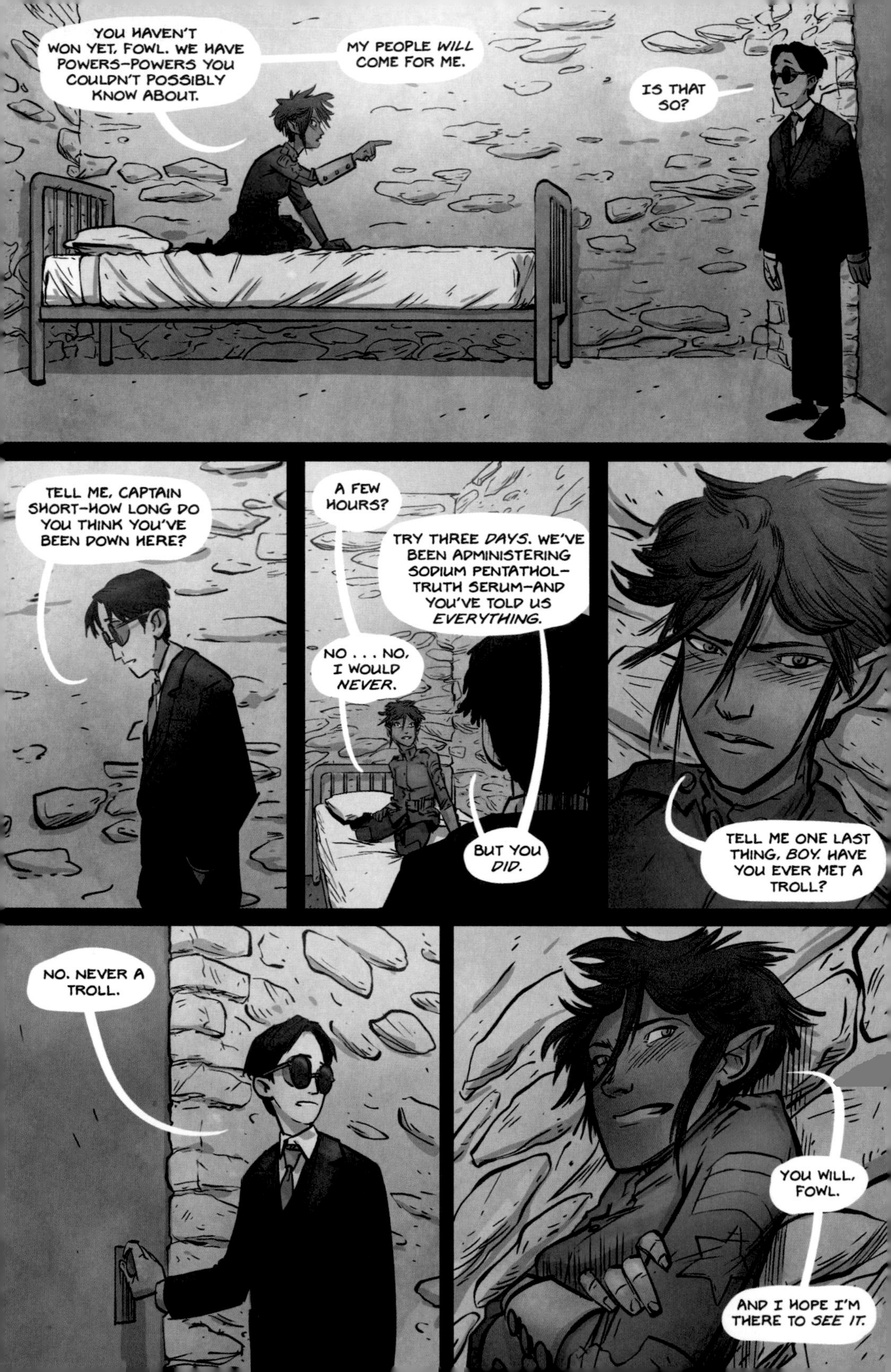
YOU HAVEN'T WON YET, FOWL. WE HAVE POWERS—POWERS YOU COULDN'T POSSIBLY KNOW ABOUT.
MY PEOPLE *WILL* COME FOR ME.
IS THAT SO?
TELL ME, CAPTAIN SHORT—HOW LONG DO YOU THINK YOU'VE BEEN DOWN HERE?
A FEW HOURS?
TRY THREE *DAYS*. WE'VE BEEN ADMINISTERING SODIUM PENTATHOL—TRUTH SERUM—AND YOU'VE TOLD US *EVERYTHING*.
NO . . . NO, I WOULD *NEVER*.
BUT YOU *DID*.
TELL ME ONE LAST THING, *BOY*. HAVE YOU EVER MET A TROLL?
NO. NEVER A TROLL.
YOU WILL, FOWL.
AND I HOPE I'M THERE TO *SEE IT*.

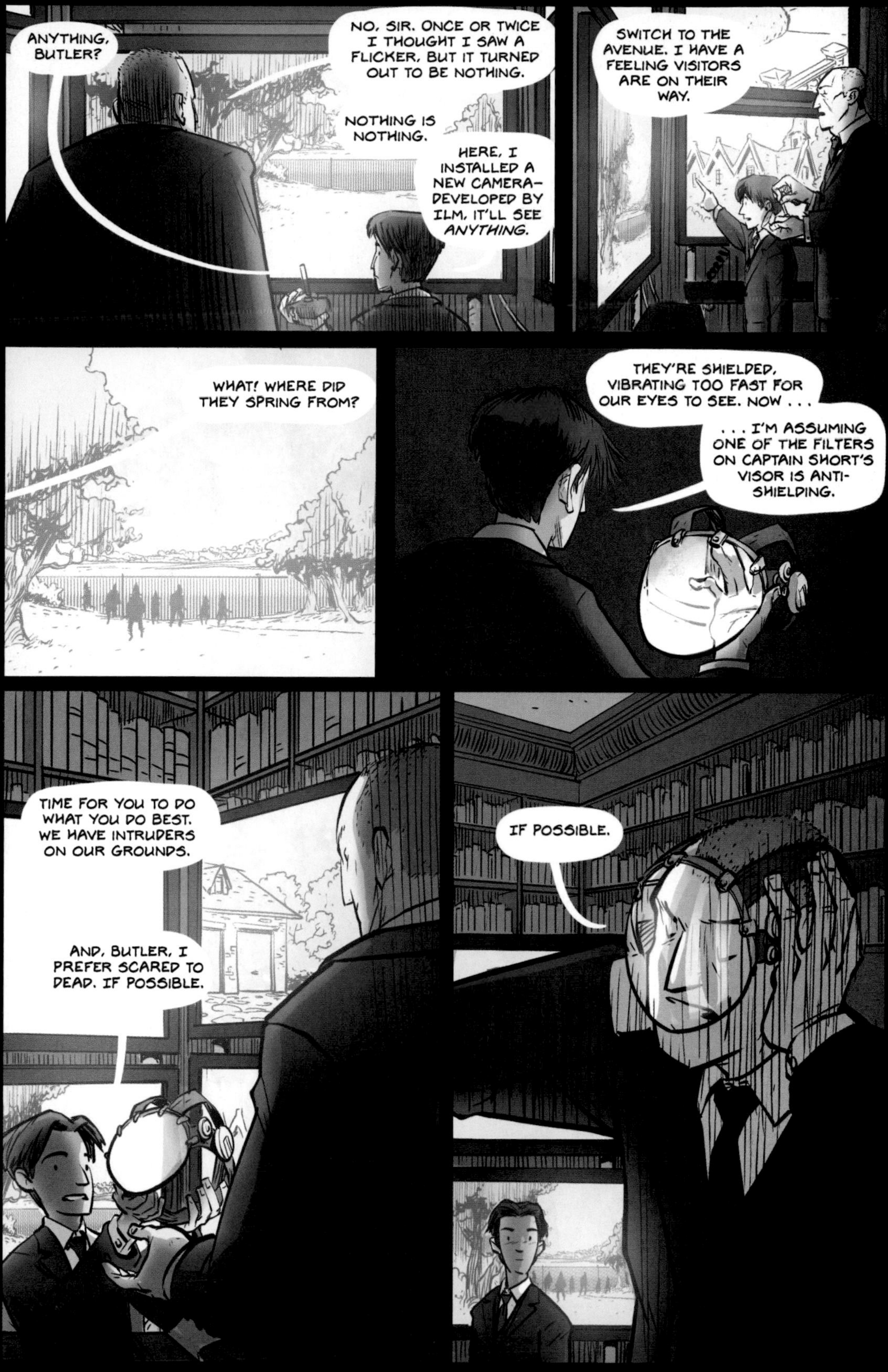
ANYTHING, BUTLER?
NO, SIR. ONCE OR TWICE I THOUGHT I SAW A FLICKER, BUT IT TURNED OUT TO BE NOTHING.
NOTHING IS NOTHING.
HERE, I INSTALLED A NEW CAMERA—DEVELOPED BY ILM, IT'LL SEE *ANYTHING*.
SWITCH TO THE AVENUE. I HAVE A FEELING VISITORS ARE ON THEIR WAY.
WHAT! WHERE DID THEY SPRING FROM?
THEY'RE SHIELDED, VIBRATING TOO FAST FOR OUR EYES TO SEE. NOW . . .
. . . I'M ASSUMING ONE OF THE FILTERS ON CAPTAIN SHORT'S VISOR IS ANTI-SHIELDING.
TIME FOR YOU TO DO WHAT YOU DO BEST. WE HAVE INTRUDERS ON OUR GROUNDS.
AND, BUTLER, I PREFER SCARED TO DEAD. IF POSSIBLE.
IF POSSIBLE.

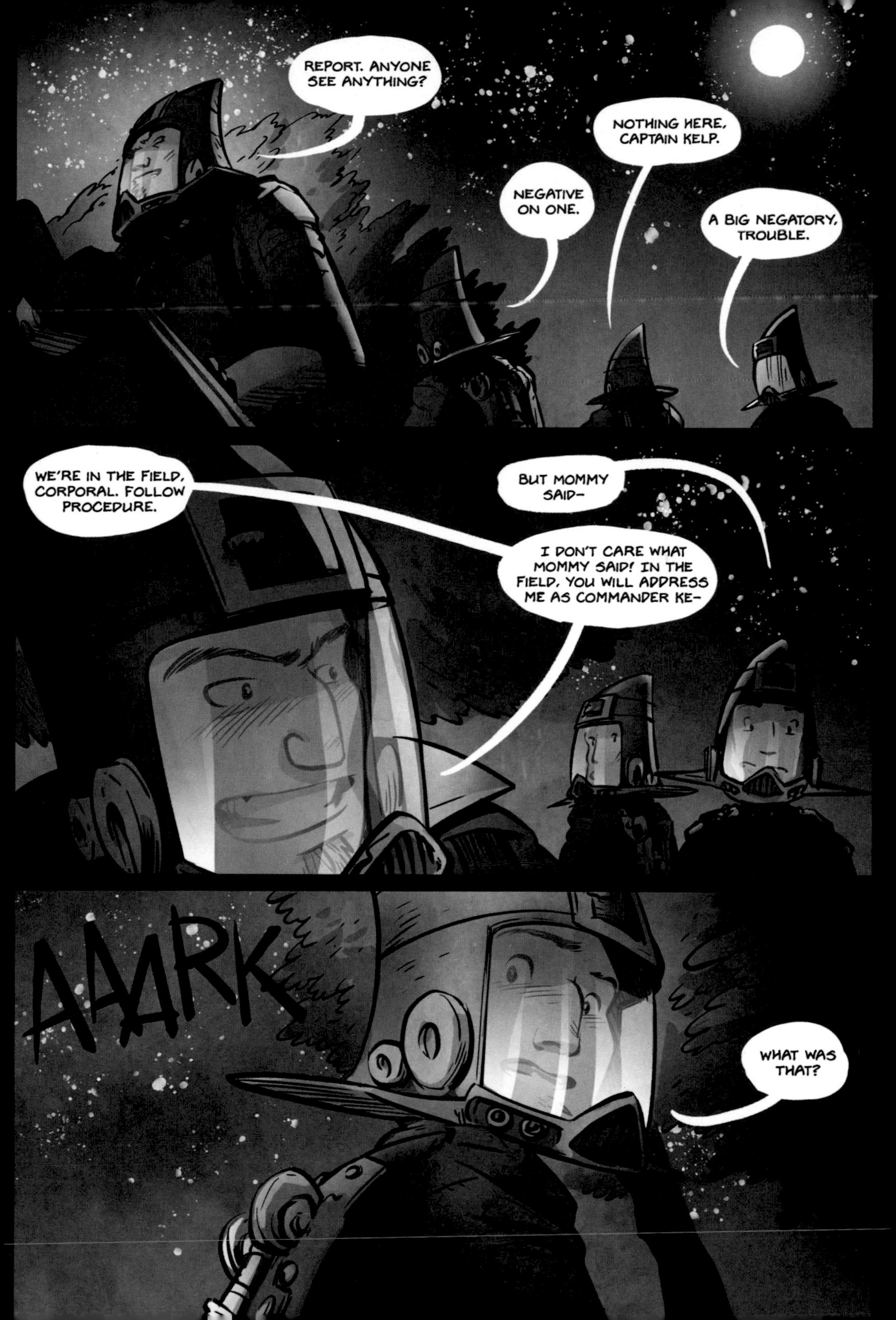
REPORT. ANYONE SEE ANYTHING?
NOTHING HERE, CAPTAIN KELP.
NEGATIVE ON ONE.
A BIG NEGATORY, TROUBLE.
WE'RE IN THE FIELD, CORPORAL. FOLLOW PROCEDURE.
BUT MOMMY SAID–
I DON'T CARE WHAT MOMMY SAID! IN THE FIELD, YOU WILL ADDRESS ME AS COMMANDER KE–
AAARK
WHAT WAS THAT?

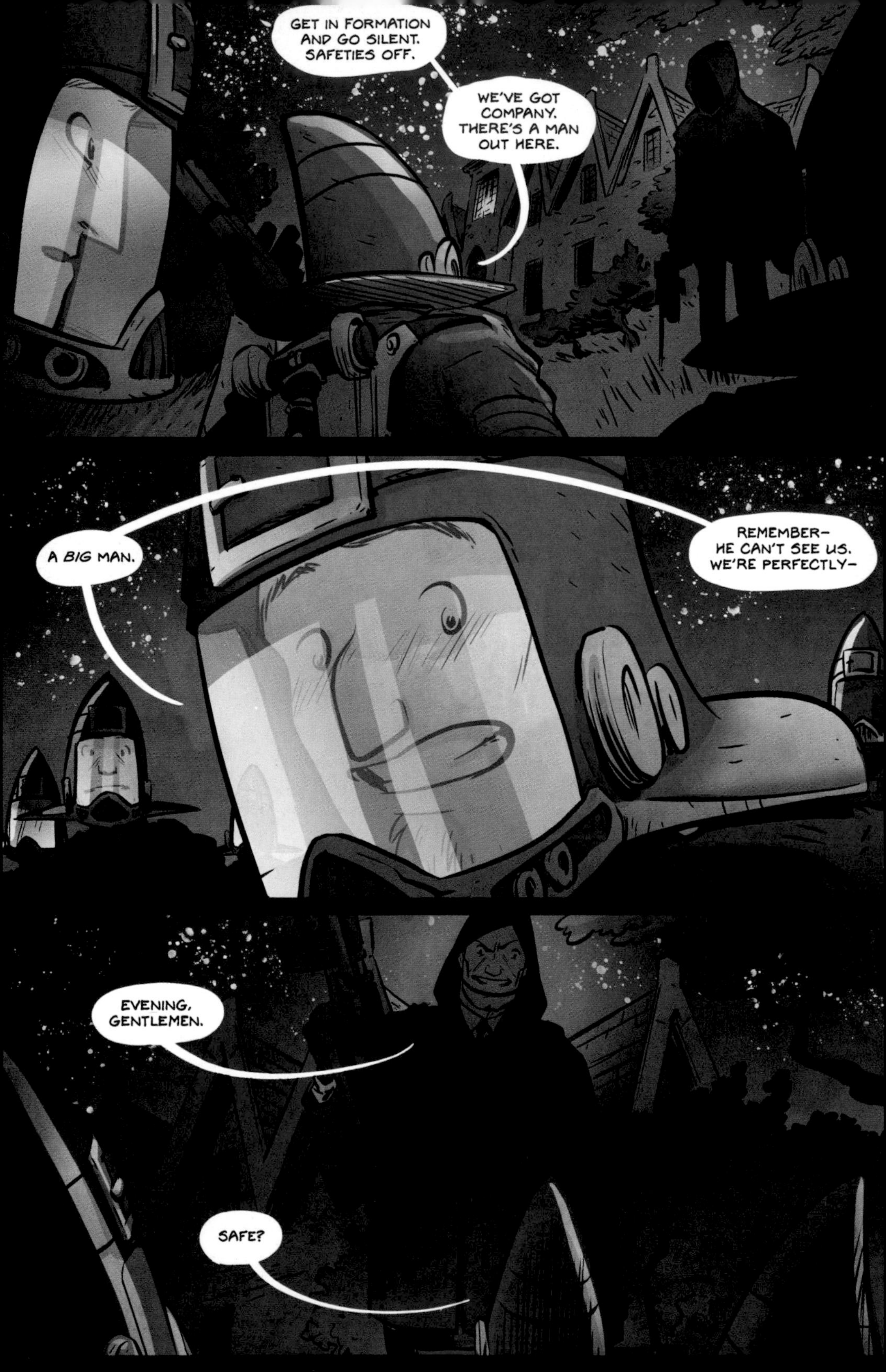
GET IN FORMATION AND GO SILENT. SAFETIES OFF.
WE'VE GOT COMPANY. THERE'S A MAN OUT HERE.
A *BIG* MAN.
REMEMBER– HE CAN'T SEE US. WE'RE PERFECTLY–
EVENING, GENTLEMEN.
SAFE?

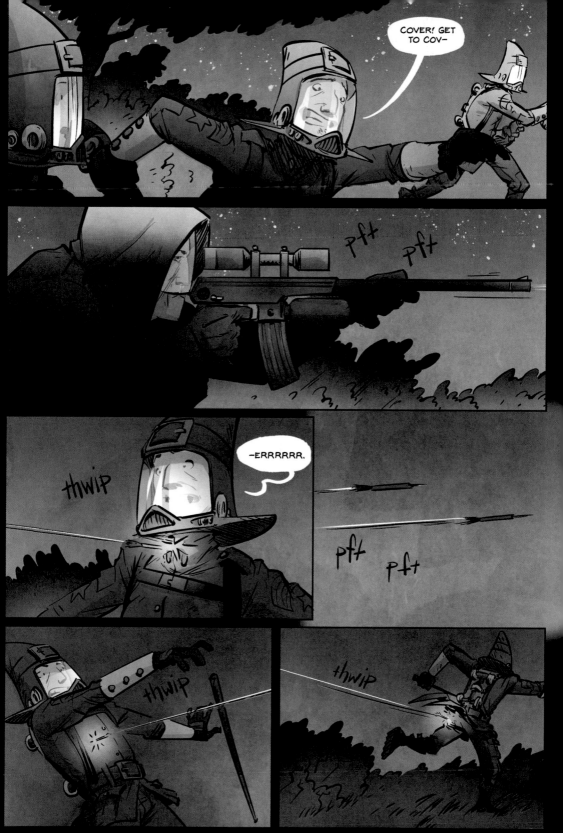

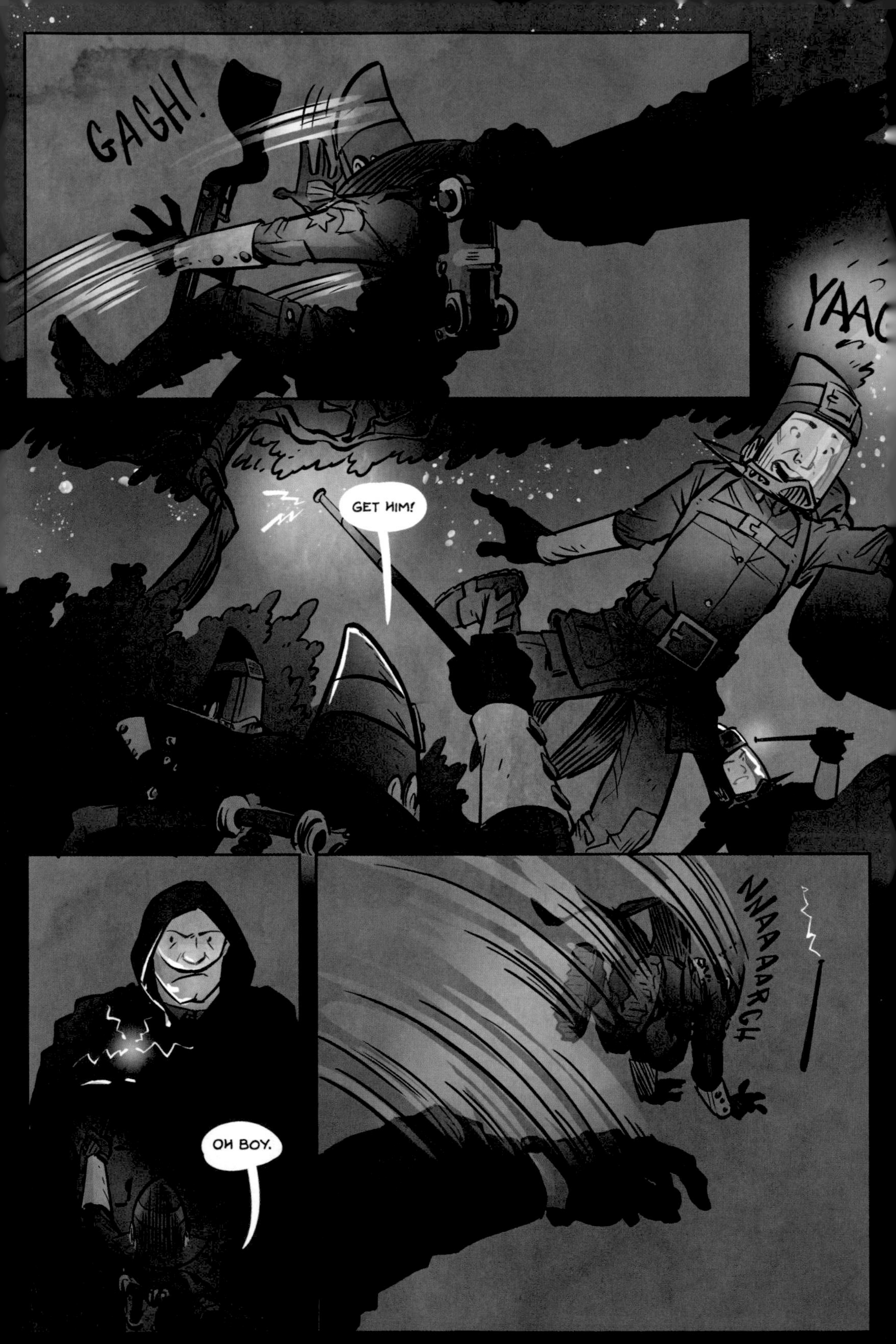
GAGH!
YAAC
GET HIM!
OH BOY.
NNAAAAARCH

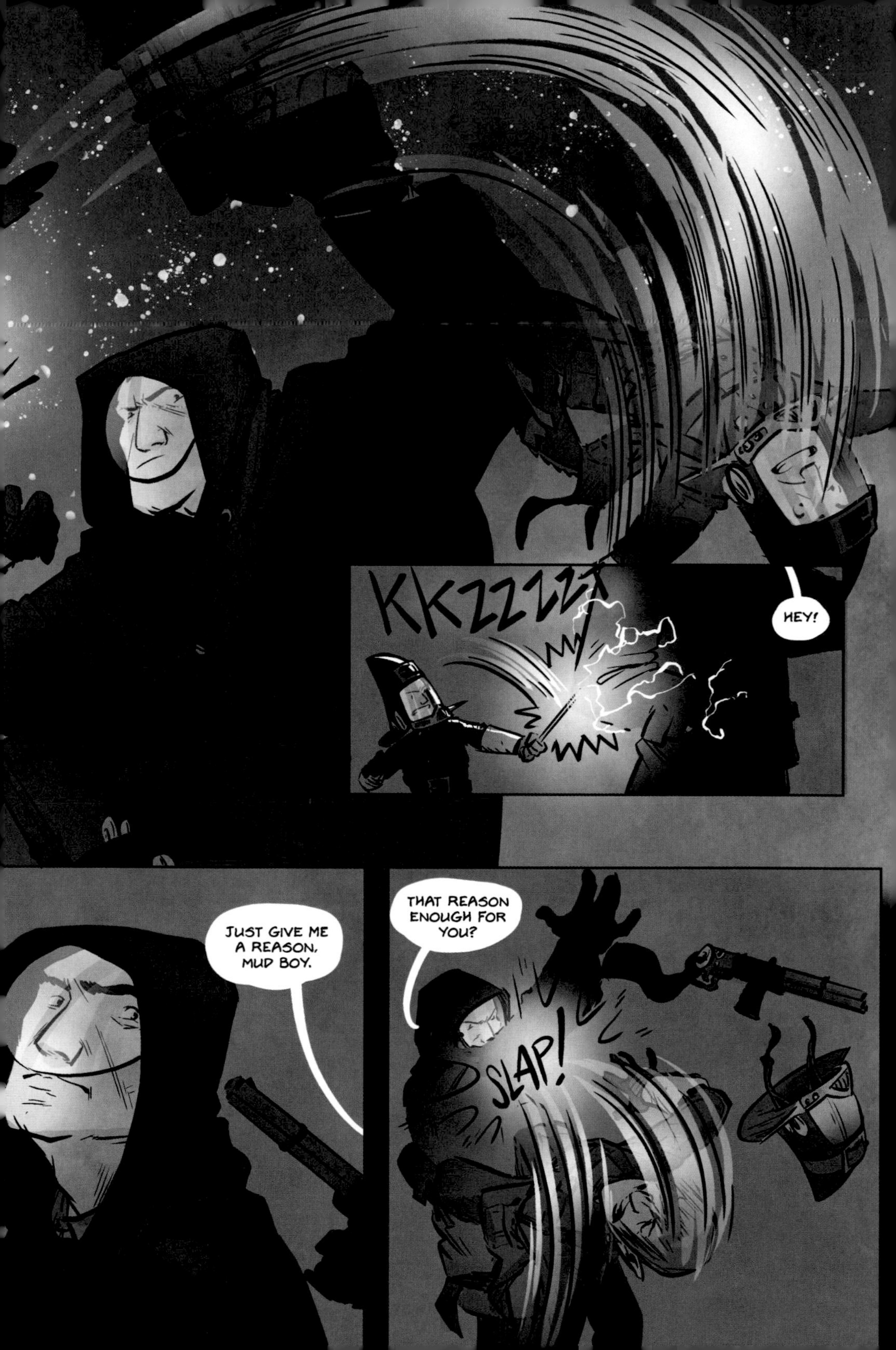
KKZZZZZT
HEY!
JUST GIVE ME A REASON, MUD BOY.
THAT REASON ENOUGH FOR YOU?
SLAP!

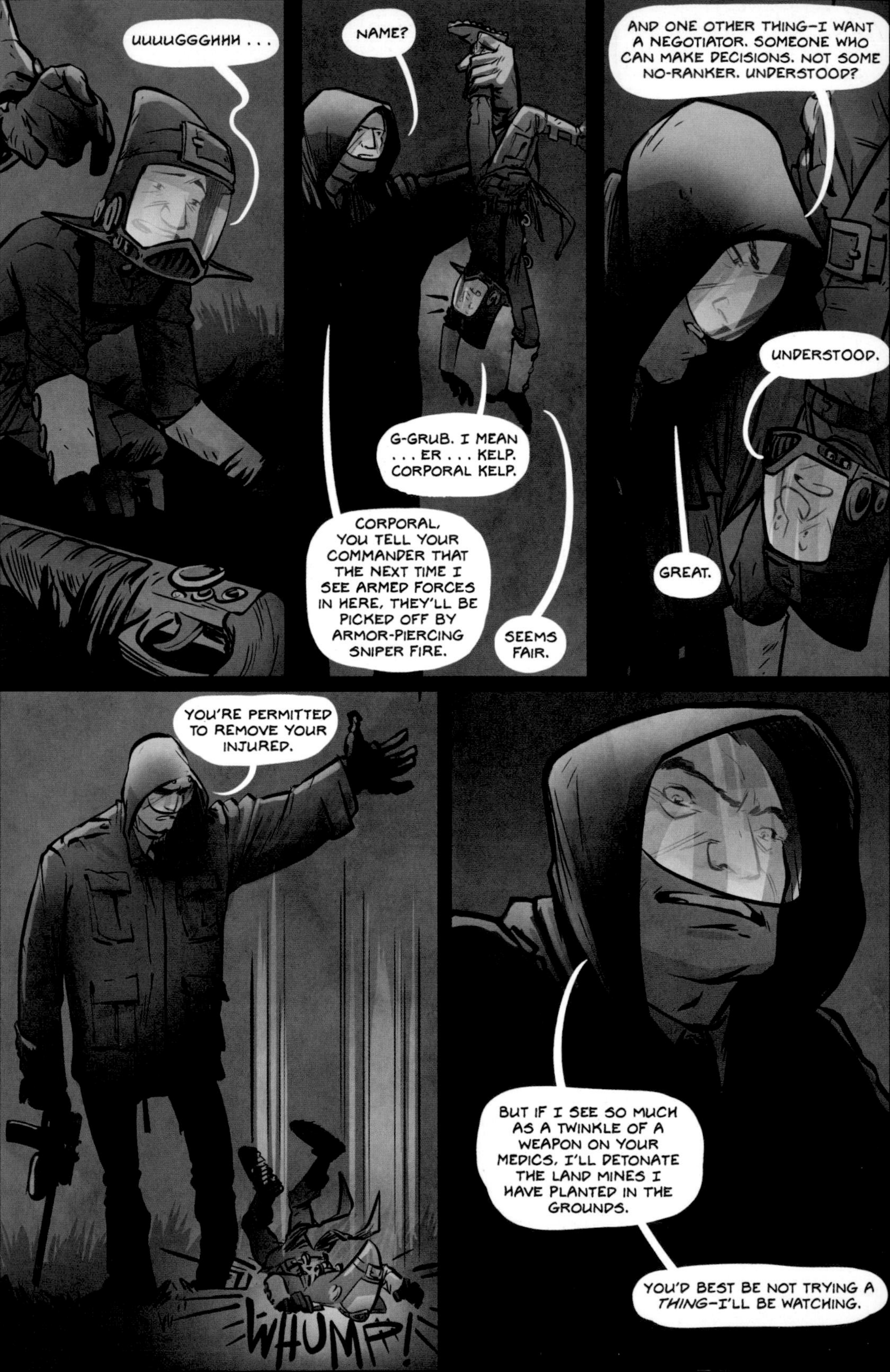
UUUUGGGHHH . . .
NAME?
G-GRUB. I MEAN . . . ER . . . KELP. CORPORAL KELP.
CORPORAL, YOU TELL YOUR COMMANDER THAT THE NEXT TIME I SEE ARMED FORCES IN HERE, THEY'LL BE PICKED OFF BY ARMOR-PIERCING SNIPER FIRE.
SEEMS FAIR.
AND ONE OTHER THING—I WANT A NEGOTIATOR. SOMEONE WHO CAN MAKE DECISIONS. NOT SOME NO-RANKER. UNDERSTOOD?
UNDERSTOOD.
GREAT.
YOU'RE PERMITTED TO REMOVE YOUR INJURED.
WHUMP!
BUT IF I SEE SO MUCH AS A TWINKLE OF A WEAPON ON YOUR MEDICS, I'LL DETONATE THE LAND MINES I HAVE PLANTED IN THE GROUNDS.
YOU'D BEST BE NOT TRYING A *THING*—I'LL BE WATCHING.

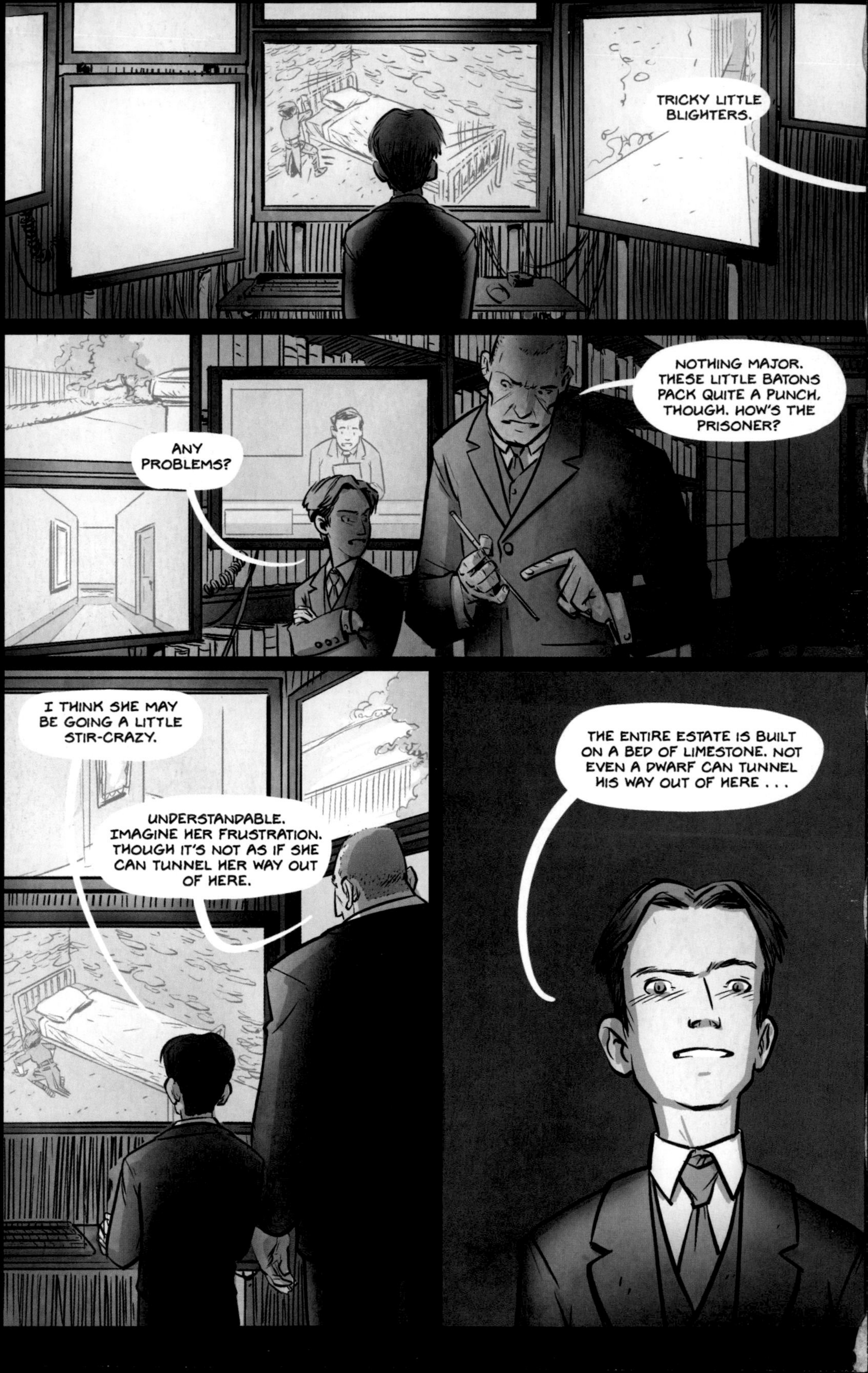
TRICKY LITTLE BLIGHTERS.
ANY PROBLEMS?
NOTHING MAJOR. THESE LITTLE BATONS PACK QUITE A PUNCH, THOUGH. HOW'S THE PRISONER?
I THINK SHE MAY BE GOING A LITTLE STIR-CRAZY.
UNDERSTANDABLE. IMAGINE HER FRUSTRATION. THOUGH IT'S NOT AS IF SHE CAN TUNNEL HER WAY OUT OF HERE.
THE ENTIRE ESTATE IS BUILT ON A BED OF LIMESTONE. NOT EVEN A DWARF CAN TUNNEL HIS WAY OUT OF HERE . . .

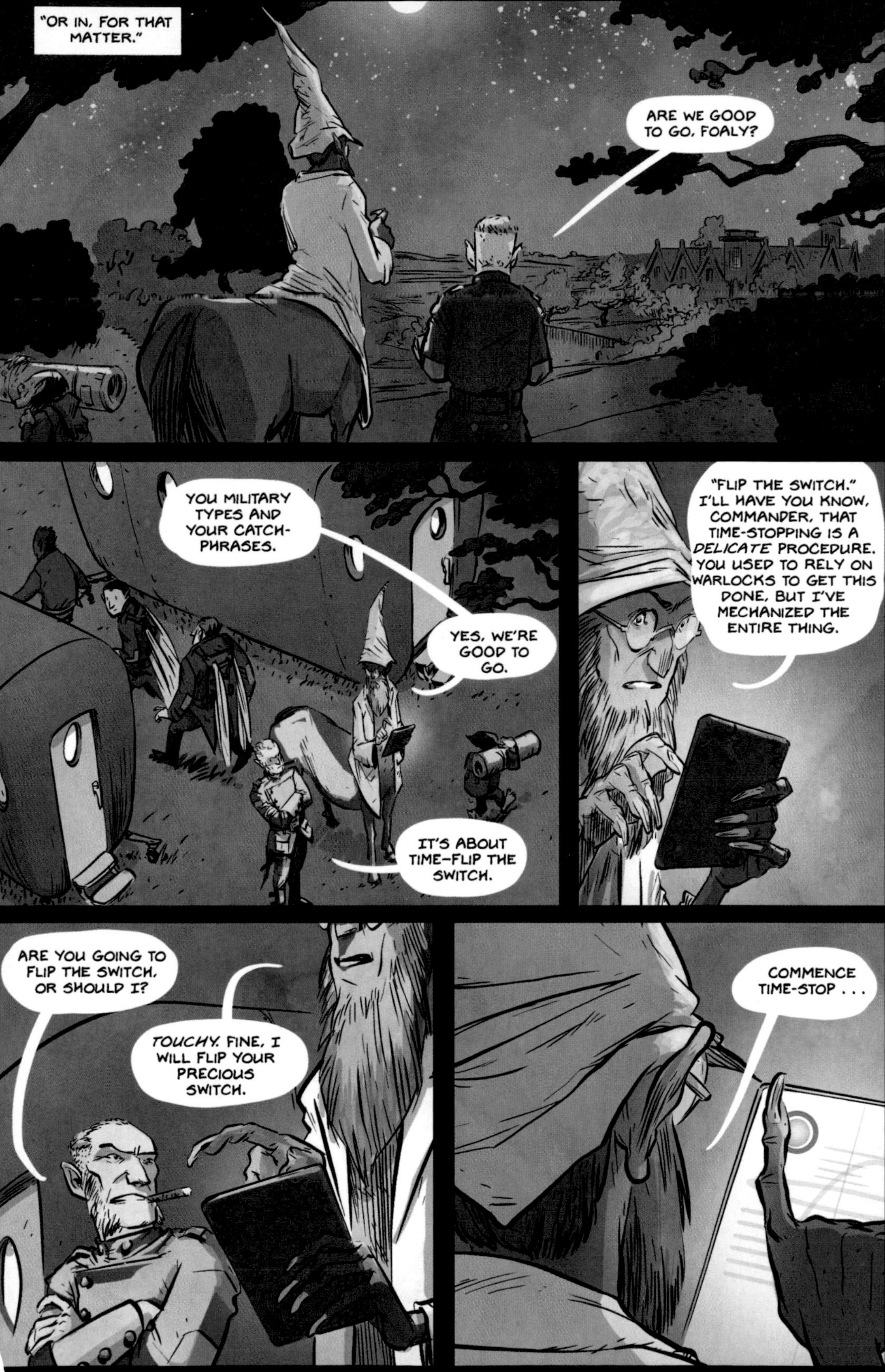
"OR IN, FOR THAT MATTER."
ARE WE GOOD TO GO, FOALY?
YOU MILITARY TYPES AND YOUR CATCH-PHRASES.
YES, WE'RE GOOD TO GO.
IT'S ABOUT TIME—FLIP THE SWITCH.
"FLIP THE SWITCH." I'LL HAVE YOU KNOW, COMMANDER, THAT TIME-STOPPING IS A *DELICATE* PROCEDURE. YOU USED TO RELY ON WARLOCKS TO GET THIS DONE, BUT I'VE MECHANIZED THE ENTIRE THING.
ARE YOU GOING TO FLIP THE SWITCH, OR SHOULD I?
TOUCHY. FINE, I WILL FLIP YOUR PRECIOUS SWITCH.
COMMENCE TIME-STOP . . .

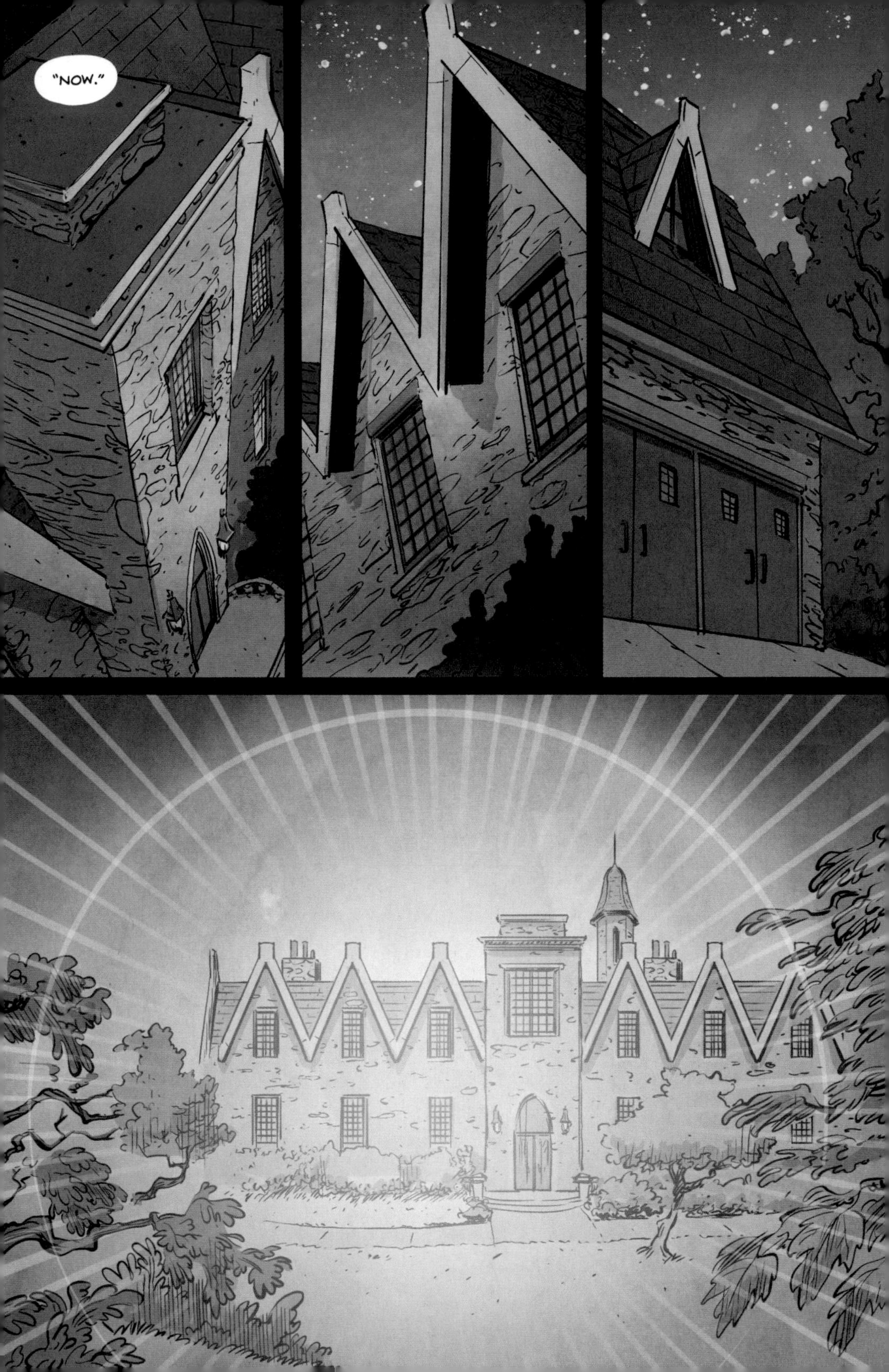
"NOW."

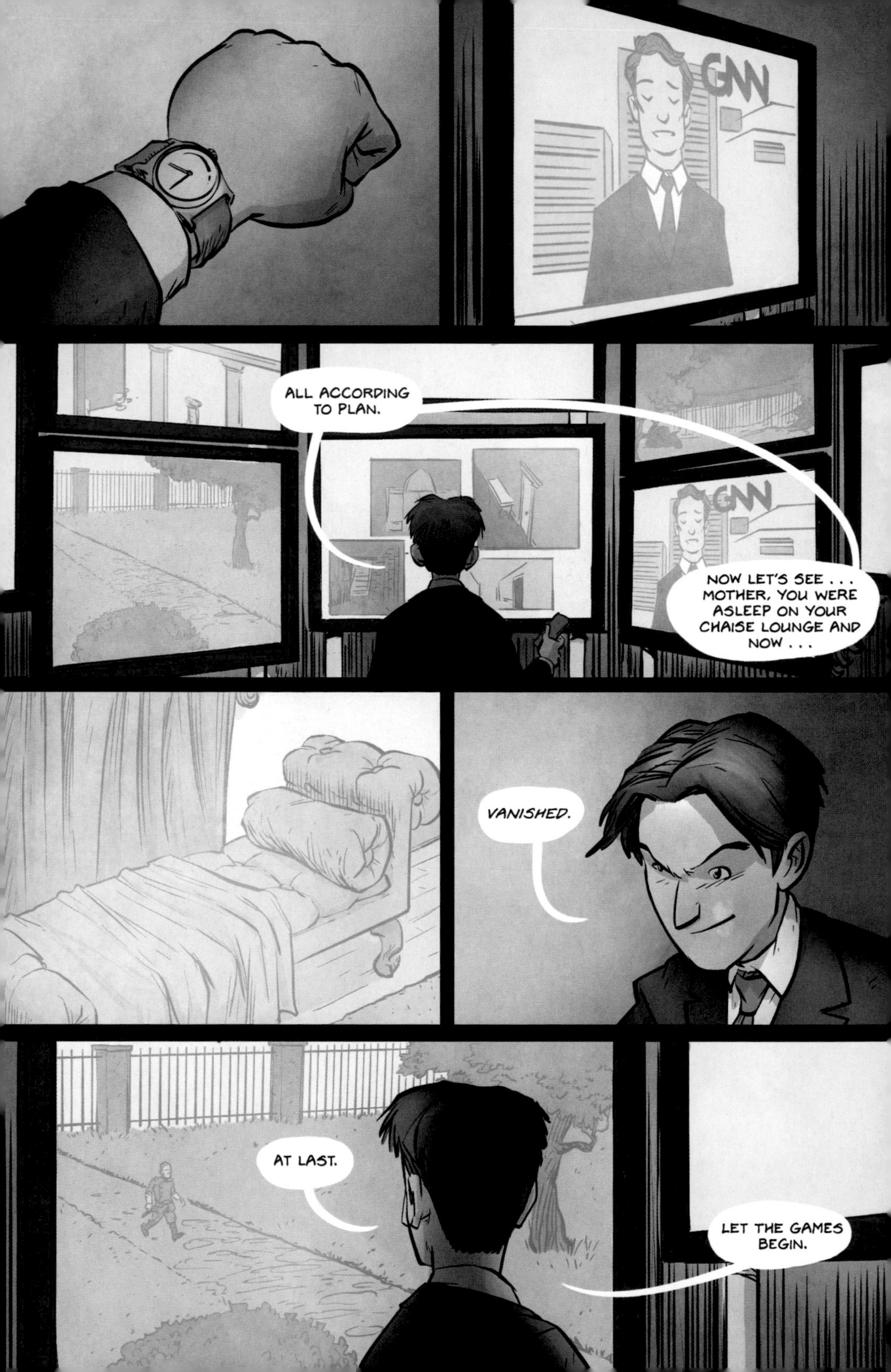
GNN
ALL ACCORDING TO PLAN.
GNN
NOW LET'S SEE . . . MOTHER, YOU WERE ASLEEP ON YOUR CHAISE LOUNGE AND NOW . . .
VANISHED.
AT LAST.
LET THE GAMES BEGIN.

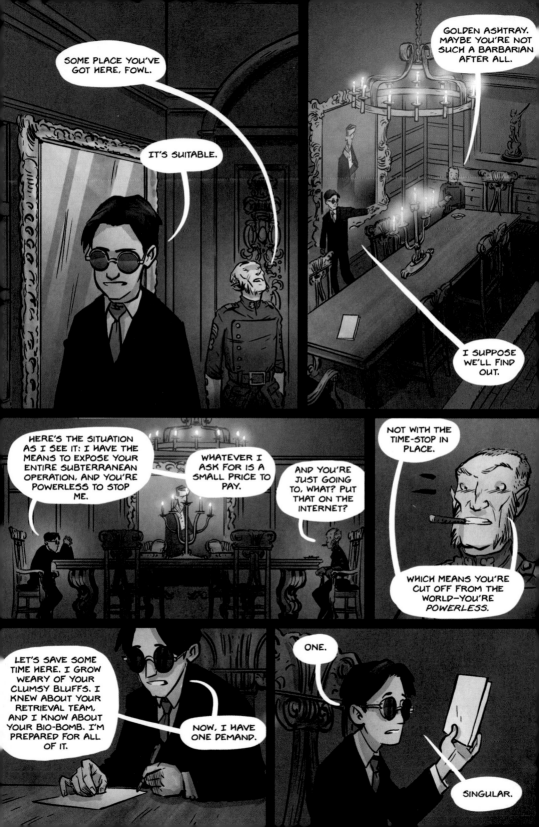

CHAPTER SEVEN

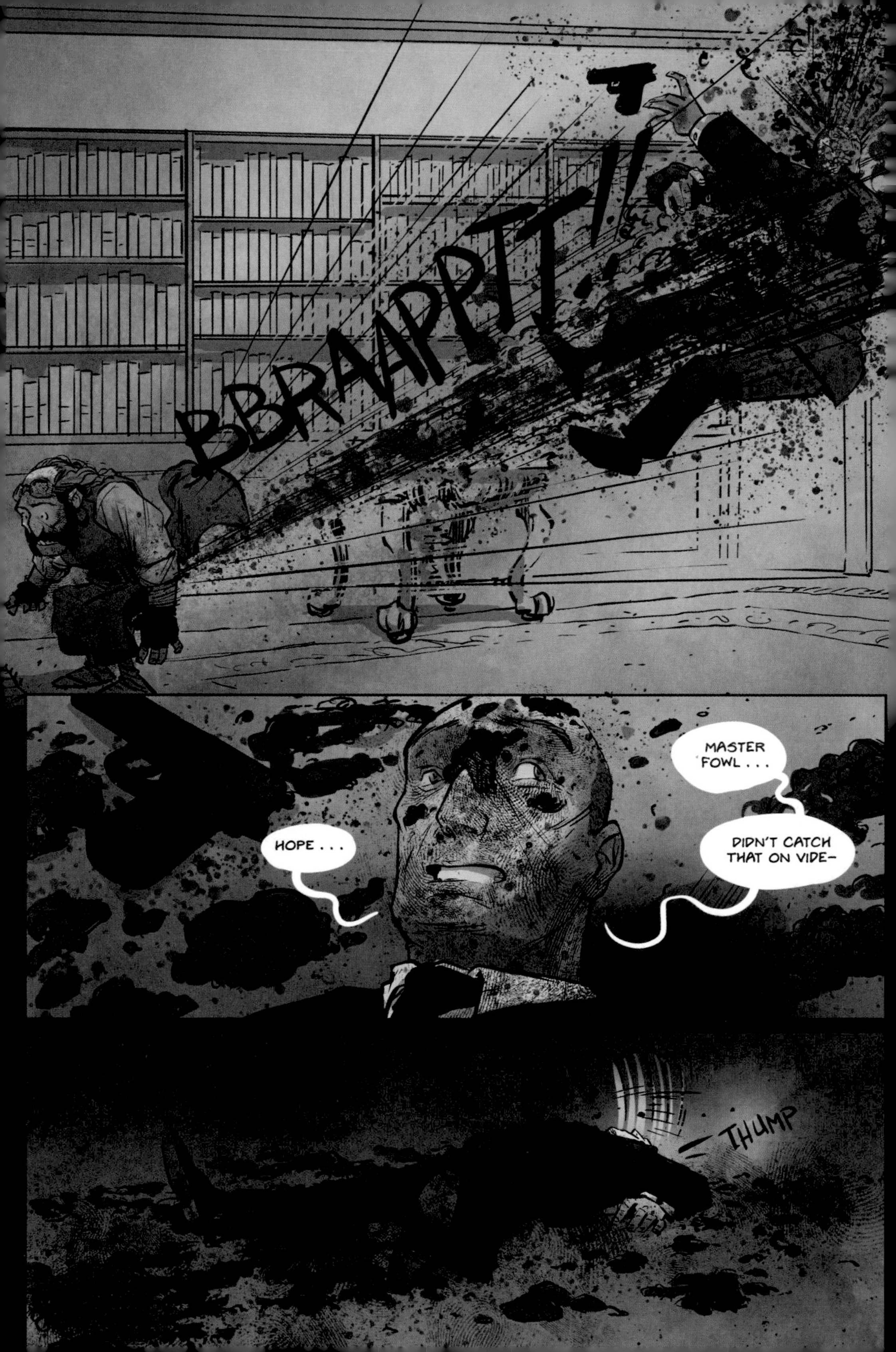
BBRAAPPTT!!
HOPE . . .
MASTER FOWL . . .
DIDN'T CATCH THAT ON VIDE–
THUMP

YOU'RE GOOD, I'LL GIVE YOU THAT, MUD MAN. BUT NO ONE TAKES A BODY BLOW FROM MULCH DIGGUMS AND STAYS ON THEIR FEET.

GET A MOVE ON, MULCH. THAT MUD MAN TOOK OUT AN ENTIRE RETRIEVAL SQUAD. I'M CERTAIN HE'D BE MORE THAN HAPPY TO REARRANGE YOUR INNARDS WHEN HE WAKES UP.

AN ENTIRE RETRIEVAL SQUAD? WELL, I'D PROBABLY BETTER—

MULCH DIGGUMS. DIDN'T EXPECT TO SEE YOU HERE.

WHAT CAN I SAY? JULES HAD A DIRTY JOB.

SOMEONE HAD TO DO IT.

IS THAT SO? AND WHAT DID YOU FIND OUT?

THIS WAS IN HIS SAFE.

A COPY OF THE BOOK! NO WONDER WE'RE IN THIS FIX.

WE'VE BEEN PLAYING INTO HIS HANDS THE ENTIRE TIME.

AND THAT MEANS MY WORK HERE IS DONE.

WHAT ARE YOU GOING TO DO?

I'M GOING TO FIND FOWL.

AND BY THE TIME I'M DONE WITH HIM, HE'S GOING TO BE BEGGING ME TO LET HIM OUT OF HIS OWN MANOR.

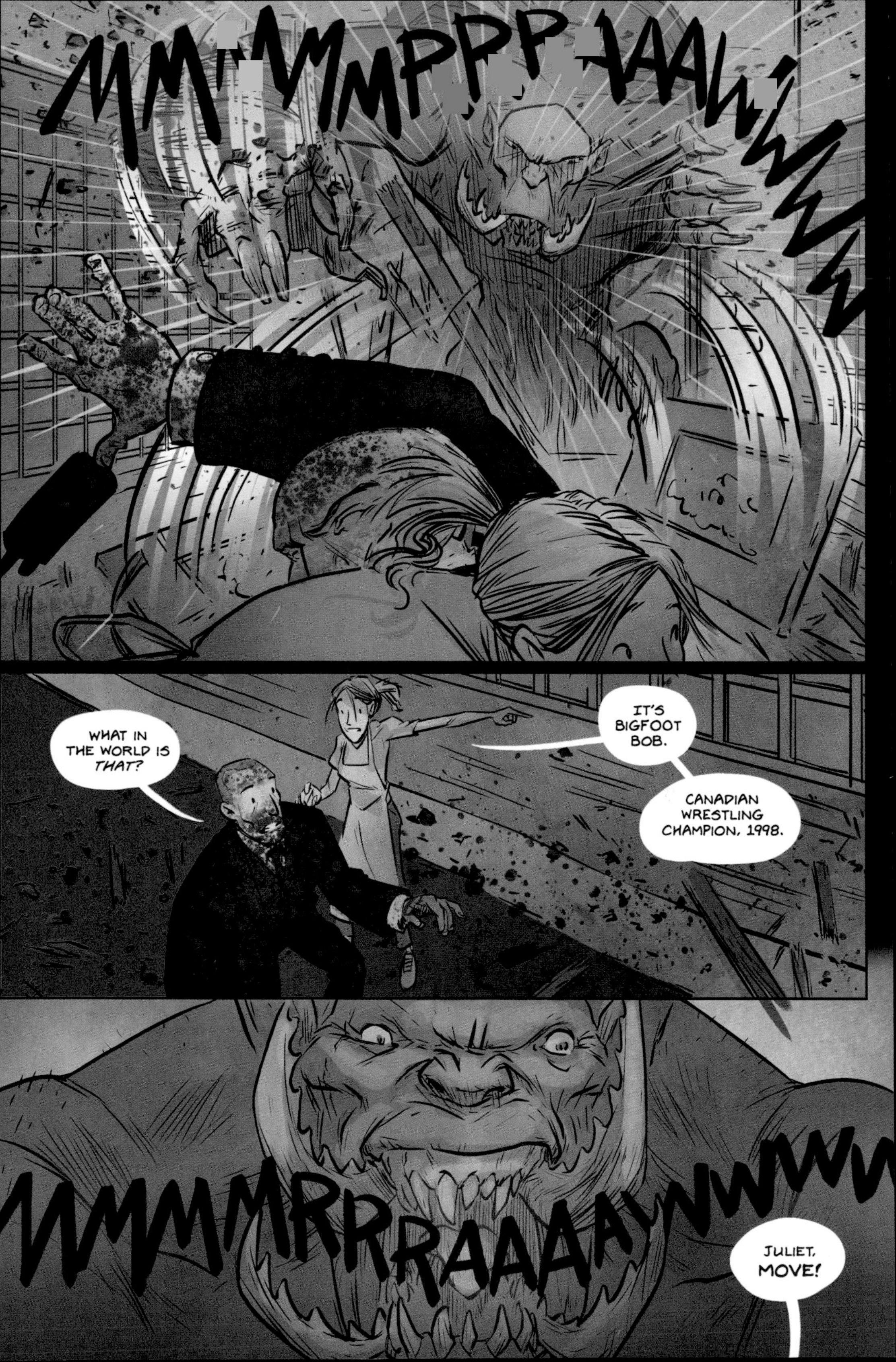
MMMMPPPAAAWWWWW
WHAT IN THE WORLD IS *THAT?*
IT'S BIGFOOT BOB.
CANADIAN WRESTLING CHAMPION, 1998.
MMMMMRRRAAAAWWWWW
JULIET, **MOVE!**

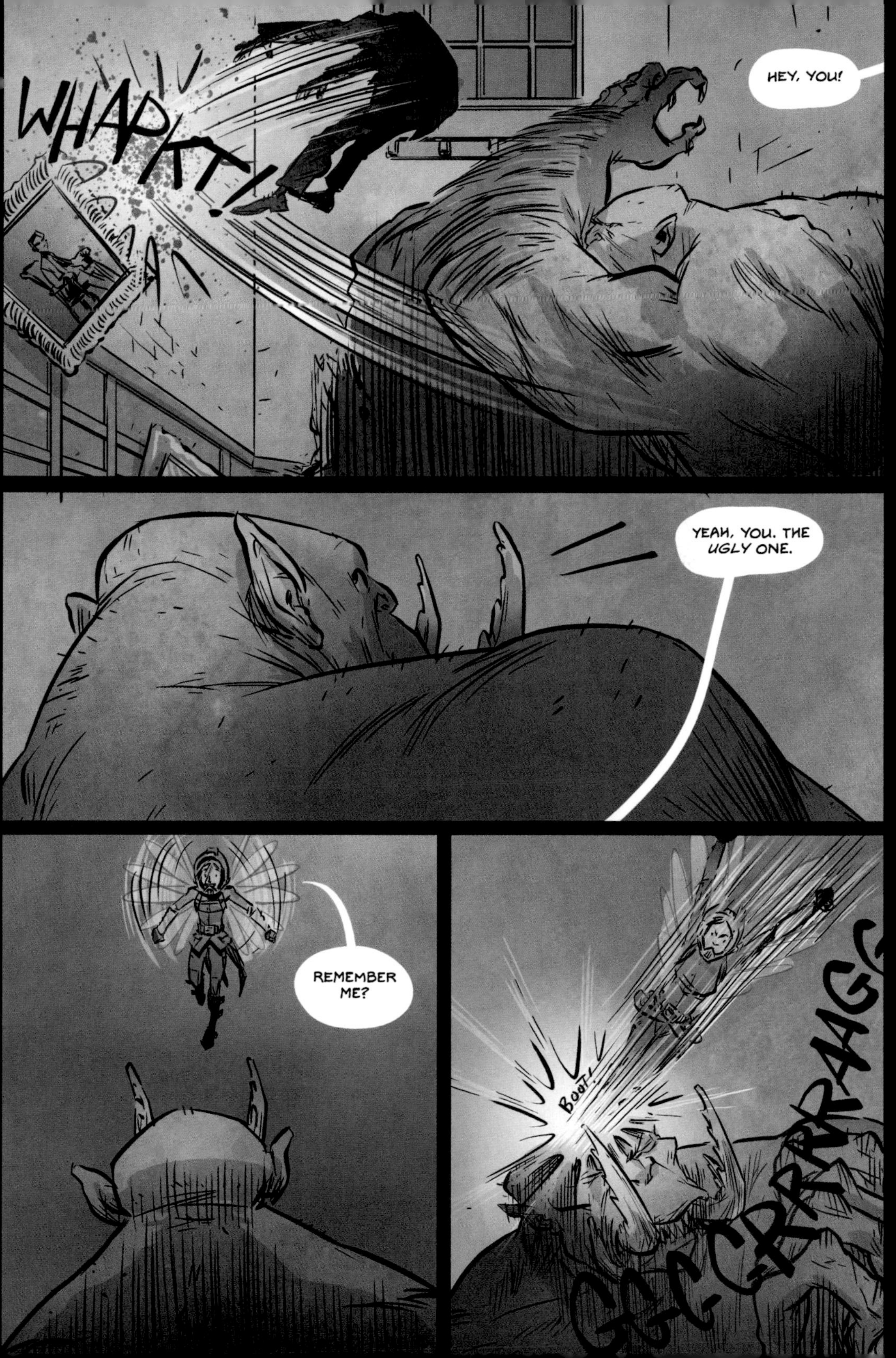
WHAPKT!!
HEY, YOU!
YEAH, YOU. THE *UGLY* ONE.
REMEMBER ME?
BOOT!
GGCRRRAAGG

THIS IS ONE *INTENSE* MATCH. MY BROTHER—HE'S FAKING IT, RIGHT?

JULIET, LISTEN TO ME. FORGET EVERYTHING I SAID BEFORE. GET OUT OF HERE.

RUN AND DON'T LOOK BA—

HOLLY—THE LIGHTS!

FOALY?

IF IT GETS ITS TUSKS IN YOU, YOU'LL BE DEAD BEFORE YOUR MAGIC CAN KICK IN.

SLASH!

AAAAHHH!

KRZZZTT

BZT

OH, DEAR.

HIT THE LIGHTS, SHORT! THAT'S AN ORDER!

I'M SORRY, COMMANDER . . .

. . . THE BEAMS ARE OFF-LINE.

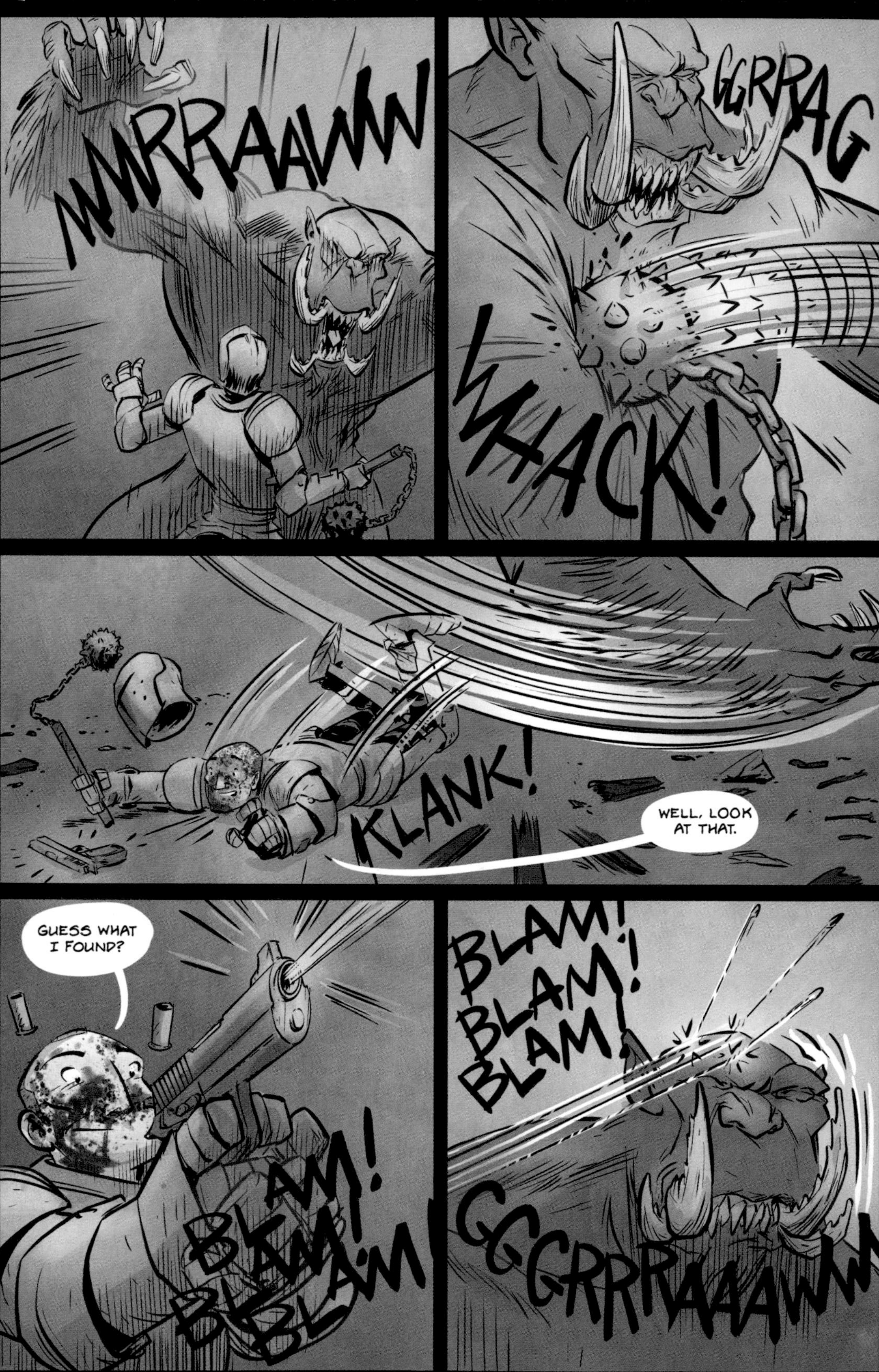
MMRRAAWW
GGRRAG
WHACK!
KLANK!
WELL, LOOK AT THAT.
GUESS WHAT I FOUND?
BLAM! BLAM! BLAM BLAM
BLAM! BLAM! BLAM! BLAM
GGGRRRRAAAWW

CHAPTER NINE

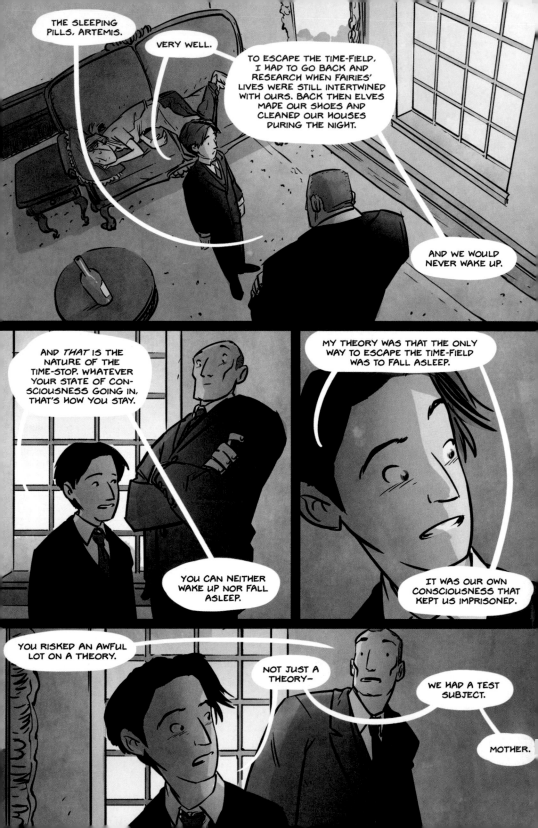

Adapted from the novel *Artemis Fowl*

Text copyright © 2019 by Eoin Colfer

Illustrations copyright © 2019 Disney Enterprises, Inc.

All rights reserved. Published by Disney • Hyperion, an imprint of
Disney Book Group. No part of this book may be reproduced or transmitted in any
form or by any means, electronic or mechanical, including photocopying, recording,
or by any information storage and retrieval system, without written permission from
the publisher. For information address Disney • Hyperion,
125 West End Avenue, New York, New York 10023.

First Hardcover Edition, June 2019

First Paperback Edition, June 2019

10 9 8 7 6 5 4 3 2 1

FAC-038091-19130

Printed in the United States of America

This book is set in Colleen Doran/Fontspring; DIN Next LT Pro, ITC Novarese Pro,
Neutraface Condensed/Monotype

Designed by Stephen Gilpin and Tyler Nevins

Library of Congress Cataloging-in-Publication Data

Names: Moreci, Michael, adapter. • Gilpin, Stephen, artist. •
Adaptation of expression: Colfer, Eoin. Artemis Fowl.
Title: Eoin Colfer's Artemis Fowl : the graphic novel /
adapted by Michael Moreci ; art by Stephen Gilpin.
Other titles: Artemis Fowl, the graphic novel
Description: First edition. • Los Angeles ; New York : Disney • Hyperion, 2019.
• Summary: When a twelve-year-old evil genius tries to restore his family
fortune by capturing a fairy and demanding a ransom in gold, the fairies
fight back with magic, technology, and a particularly nasty troll.
Identifiers: LCCN 2018028370• ISBN 9781368043144 (hardcover)
ISBN 9781368043700 (pbk.) • Subjects: LCSH: Graphic novels. • CYAC: Graphic novels. •
Fairies—Fiction. • Kidnapping—Fiction. • Magic—Fiction. • Mothers and sons—Fiction. •
England—Fiction. • Classification: LCC PZ7.7.M658 Eoi 2019 • DDC 741.5/942—dc23
LC record available at https://lccn.loc.gov/2018028370

Visit www.DisneyBooks.com